Could she say yes? Rafael somehow made the decision sound so straight-forward. He made everything seem possible.

But then he had no thought or care for the life she had made for herself in England. Built up so painstakingly, brick by brick, from the demolition rubble of their marriage. She had finally reached the stage where she felt financially stable and emotionally settled. Most of the time anyway.

Could Lottie really take this enormous gamble and throw caution, common sense and self-preservation to the wind? Hurl them up into the blue sky and watch to see where they fell? The same blue sky that Rafael had fallen from—that had brought her here in the first place.

It was so tempting.

Rafael waited, as if sensing that words were no longer needed. So close now she could feel the soft whisper of his breath against her face, feel herself weakening beneath the unbearable scrutiny of his gaze and the lethal, sensual intoxication of his nearness.

Sitting up very straight, Lottie pushed back her shoulders and mirrored his penetrating stare. This was her decision and she was going to make it.

The answering ⬚⬚⬚⬚⬚⬚⬚⬚⬚⬚⬚⬚⬚ ntense that ⬚⬚⬚⬚⬚⬚⬚⬚⬚⬚⬚⬚⬚⬚ denly dry

'My

Andie Brock started inventing imaginary friends around the age of four and is still doing that today— only now the sparkly fairies have made way for spirited heroines and sexy heroes.

Thankfully she now has some real friends, as well as a husband and three children, plus a grumpy but lovable cat.

Andie lives in Bristol, and when not actually writing could well be plotting her next passionate romance story.

This is Andie's stunning debut—
we hope you love it as much as we do!

Did you know this is also available as an eBook?
Visit www.millsandboon.co.uk

THE LAST HEIR
OF MONTERRATO

BY
ANDIE BROCK

MILLS & BOON

Published in Great Britain 2015
by Mills & Boon, an imprint of Harlequin (UK) Limited,
Eton House, 18-24 Paradise Road, Richmond, Surrey, TW9 1SR

© 2015 Andie Brock

ISBN: 978-0-263-24830-2

THE LAST HEIR
OF MONTERRATO

For my mum. Who would have been very proud.

CHAPTER ONE

IT WAS THE scar that halted Lottie in the doorway. A thin, livid wound, it sliced down from his brow, skipping over the eye socket before continuing an inch along his cheekbone. The sight of it clutched at her stomach, weighted her feet to the floor.

'Rafael?'

Silence stretched tightly between them as they stared at each other across the dark panelled office.

'Charlotte.'

'How...how are you?'

'Still alive.' As he eased himself to stand against the edge of the desk his voice was cold, flat. 'As you can see.'

'Yes. Indeed.' Lottie swallowed. Upright now, he stood with his hands splayed on either side of him, fingertips anchoring him to the desk. 'I was very sorry—to hear about the accident, I mean.'

'Thank you.' His clipped reply snipped at her words, clearly designed to stop any outpourings of sentiment.

Not that she intended to show him any, of course. She knew she wasn't here to display any sort of concern, express any sympathy. Rafael wasn't the kind of man to tolerate such emotions. Especially from her.

She watched as he moved out from behind the desk and walked stiffly towards her, tall and rigid in a sober grey suit, his height towering over her as they came together. For a second they stood there, like repelling magnets, until Rafael bent forward to brush her cheek once, twice, three times. Lottie closed her eyes as she felt the whisper of his breath, the touch of his skin; *him.*

He pulled away immediately, leaving her staring up at his injuries.

Scratches of various lengths and depths crisscrossed his face and a purple bruise spread colourfully down one side. The scar, Lottie now realised, resembled the lash of a whip. That didn't help at all.

'So...um...your face...?' She knew she shouldn't go on about it, that he would hate her even mentioning it, but she needed reassurance, needed to stop looking at him as if she was witnessing a pig having its throat cut. 'I assume the injuries are quite superficial?'

'You assume correctly.'

'And the rest of your body?' His unnerving stare stupidly made her blush. So much for trying to appear detached. She gave a small cough. 'I mean, what other injuries do you have?'

'All fairly consistent with someone who has plummeted twelve thousand feet from the sky.'

'I'm sure.' Lottie pulled a face at the idiocy of her question. How many people had fallen twelve thousand feet and lived to tell the tale? Anyway, she already knew the extent of his injuries; it had all been there in the newspaper article: punctured lung, dislocated shoulder, three cracked ribs. 'Did you ever find out...what went wrong? Why your parachute didn't open?'

'Misfortune, fate—call it what you like.' Rafael shrugged his shoulders as if already bored with the subject. 'It's of no consequence now.'

'No, I suppose not.' But despite his casual dismissal

Lottie didn't doubt that the accident had been thoroughly investigated. And if someone had been found responsible it would be their own life they should be worrying about now. 'But you were very lucky, as it turned out.'

'Lucky?' His tone suggested otherwise.

'I mean lucky that a tree broke your fall. It could have been so much worse.'

'True.' His reply was deadpan. 'I could have been dead.'

'Ha!' Why was she laughing? Nothing about this was the least bit funny.

It was pure, unmitigated torture.

She had prepared herself, of course, endlessly rehearsed how she would behave, what she would say when faced with Rafael again. She'd still been running through her calm and measured responses on the aeroplane over here, her twitching lips attracting the attention of her nosy nine-year-old neighbour. She had bullied herself into believing that she was ready. That she could cope—survive this one last meeting.

But as she looked at him now, past the recently inflicted injuries to the man beneath, the man she had fallen so madly in love with, all her confident convictions seemed to slide away. She remembered every tiny detail of his face. The thick, untidy brows that arrowed above almond-shaped deep brown eyes. The harsh sweep of his jaw-line, the square chin where a small cleft nestled, dark with stubble.

Yep, she remembered everything. She wished she didn't.

'Well, thank goodness for that tree, eh?' Shifting her position, she crossed one leg in front of the other, the balletic pose spoiled by the hand that was shoved deep into the pocket of her jeans. Her voice sounded hideously chirpy but it did at least mask her desire to ask where this tree was, so she could throw herself on its dirty roots and thank it for saving Rafael's life. 'I'm so glad it was in the right place.'

A curl of disdain twitched Rafael's perfectly formed lip. 'How nice that you should care.'

It didn't sound nice—not at all. Everything about his cold, sarcastic manner, the harsh light in his eyes, the formal, brittle posture, was telling her one thing. He hated her.

If Lottie had hoped that time had washed over their past, smoothed the jagged edges of her actions, time had seriously let her down. It had been two years since she had left, wrenched herself away from the wreckage of their marriage and fled back to England. But being back at Palazzo Monterrato, staring at Rafael now, she knew that those two years were as nothing. The atmosphere between them was almost as horrendous, as harrowingly painful, as the day she had left.

'Of course I care.' Something about the absurdity of his comment made her want at least to attempt to put the record straight. Make him see that, despite her all too convincing performance, she wasn't all bad. 'That will never change.'

'Very touching, I'm sure.' Rafael's words sliced through her tentative confession. 'But your misplaced sympathy is of no interest to me.' He moved back to his side of the desk. 'You are here because there is an important matter I need to discuss with you. Please, sit down.'

Lottie took a seat opposite him, her rapped knuckles clasped in her lap, her back very straight. She knew what was coming; she had been waiting for this ever since she had received his email.

It had been just another afternoon at work when she had opened her inbox and there it had been: a message from Rafael Revaldi. To see his name like that, out of the blue, had sent a hot flush of panic through her body. She had had to count to three before she'd even dared open it, darting a look at the only other people in the exclusive London art gallery—a whispering gay couple, admiring a vast canvas they were never going to buy—in case they had noticed her alarm.

The curt, dictatorial message had stated that it was necessary for them to meet; two different dates for the following week had been marked for her consideration and flight tickets would be emailed on receipt of her confirmation. As her mind had whizzed with the flurry of possibilities it had quickly settled on the cold blanket of truth behind the message. He wanted a divorce.

Tipping her chin, Lottie forced herself to meet his gaze, affecting as much detachment as she could muster, determined to be strong now. 'I know why I'm here. Let me assure you that I am as keen to get this over and done with as you are. I have no intention of being difficult, of trying to prolong the situation.'

There was a dangerous flash in Rafael's eyes before they narrowed to conceal anything further. He said nothing.

'If you have already had the papers drawn up...' she was babbling now, in her hurry to get this over with '...and it's just a matter of signature I can sign straight away and—'

'Let me stop you there, Charlotte.' Raising a hand, he silenced her, a gold cufflink glinting in the low afternoon light. 'I have no idea what you are talking about.'

'The divorce, of course.' Lottie felt heat rising to her cheeks at the very use of the dreaded d word. 'I know I am here because you want a divorce.'

Rafael leant forward, the fine fabric of his jacket pulling taut against his broad shoulders as his elbows rested on the desk in front of him, his hands linked.

'And what makes you think I want a divorce?'

Lottie looked down, picking at the skin around her fingernails. 'Because it's been two years.' She could feel his eyes boring into the crown of her bent head and forced herself to look up and confront him. 'And two years is the legal time necessary to apply for a consensual divorce.'

'And you think *that* is why I have brought you here?' His words were mocking, biting.

'Well, isn't it?'

'Believe me, Charlotte, if and when I want a divorce it will happen. The vagaries of English law are of no interest to me.'

Of course, Lottie corrected herself, how foolish of her. She should have known that as far as Rafael was concerned laws were something other people abided by. He had the power and the cunning to circumnavigate them, adapt them to his own needs.

Quickly she scanned the face of the man opposite her, afraid to let her eyes linger in any one spot for fear of being unable to drag them away again. He presented a cold, harsh picture, with the damaged skin pulled tight across the sculpted planes of his cheeks and jawline.

Why was he denying it? Did he get some perverse pleasure from watching her squirm? If so, that pleasure had to be locked deep inside him, for she had never seen him look more severe, more forbidding. She *knew* he wanted to divorce her; receiving that email had only confirmed the bleak realisation that had been silently gnawing away at her for nearly three weeks now. Ever since she had innocently stumbled across that online newspaper article.

Rafael Revaldi, Conte di Monterrato, cheats death in terrifying skydiving accident.

The words of the headline had made the cappuccino shake in her hand, the bite of sandwich turn into a ball of concrete in her mouth. Gripping the computer mouse, she had frantically read on, desperate to find as much information as she could, as fast as she could, her hitherto steadfast vow not to type Rafael's name anywhere near the search engine box vanishing like vapour in the air.

But there had been way too much information. The Italian celebrity magazines were positively bursting with sensational details about the daredevil Conte who had plunged twelve thousand feet to earth and miraculously lived to tell the tale. Any legitimate concern had soon morphed into a gluttonous feeding frenzy to find out every little bit of gossip about him that she could. And what she'd discovered—apart from the predictable images of him scaling mountains or kayaking over waterfalls—were women. Beautiful, eligible women. Glued to his side as they smiled at charity galas, shook hands with dignitaries, walked beside him on the red carpet. And all of them had one thing in common: a vice-tight grip on his arm and a look in their eye that said, *Tonight he's mine and I intend to keep it that way.*

Any fanciful ideas Lottie might have had about jumping on a plane to be with him, to make sure for herself that he was really okay, had been wrenched away from her there and then as she'd stared at the frozen smiles of those women. They were all the proof she needed that Rafael had moved on. That she had no place in his life any more.

Which was fine. Even if being here with him now, talking about severing all ties with him, sliced through her like a cold blade. She just needed to remind herself how far she had come. Yes, her life was finally back on track, and that realisation stiffened her resolve.

Pushing back her shoulders, she attempted a haughty glare to match his sullen one. She needed an explanation.

'So if, as you seem to be implying, I'm *not* here because

you want a divorce, perhaps you would do me the courtesy of telling me exactly why I *am* here?'

A heavy silence hung between them, marked out by the weary ticking of a long-case clock somewhere in the shadows.

'You are here because I have something to ask of you.' He paused, a muscle twitching beneath the hard, tight mask of authority.

Lottie watched as he uncharacteristically twiddled a gold pen between strong, tapered fingers so that it tapped—first one end, then the other—lightly on the desk before him. She found she was holding her breath at the absurd realisation that Rafael was nervous.

'I think we should try again.'

Shock ricocheted through Lottie's body. And despite herself—despite everything—the see-saw carrying her heart flew into the air.

'Try again?' Her mouth was so dry the words sounded shrivelled.

'Yes. I think we should try again. For a baby.'

The see-saw crashed down to the ground with a shuddering thump.

'A *baby*?' She hadn't meant it to sound so sneery, so nasty, but incredulity had taken her words and twisted them with bitterness.

'Yes, a *baby*, Charlotte. I see no reason why we shouldn't at least consider the idea.'

No reason at all, Lottie reasoned numbly, other than the fact that their marriage had been a disaster, he hadn't spoken to her for two years and he obviously still hated her guts. 'Why would you even think…?'

'I have found a new IVF specialist—someone in Iran,' Rafael continued with baffling logic. 'He knows the situation—that we still have one frozen embryo. He is very confident that this time it will work, that this time we will succeed.'

An Iranian IVF specialist? What on earth was going on here? Despite the controlled voice, the even tone, the powerful sense of conviction running through him was clearly, disturbingly unmistakable.

She had seen it before, of course. Rafael's determination to get her pregnant. But that had been in a previous life, before they had split up. After Seraphina had died.

Born at just twenty-five weeks, their daughter had only lived for a few precious hours. The trauma of the accident, followed by premature labour and a complicated birth was now little more than a foggy blur—almost as if it had happened to somebody else. But the pain of watching their tiny daughter's vain struggle for life would stay with Lottie for ever.

When Seraphina had finally died, and the clips and wires had been removed from her perfect, breathless body, Lottie had gazed at the still warm bundle in her arms, brushed an oversized finger against the soft down of her cheeks, convinced that nothing could be worse than this, that this was the bottom of the blackest pit. But fate had had one more arrow in its quiver. It seemed that the accident meant she would never be able to conceive naturally again—that IVF was their only hope of ever having another child.

Rafael had set about making it happen with a tenacious stubbornness that had bordered on obsession. They had embarked upon a series of IVF treatments, none of which had worked, and after each crushing disappointment it had seemed he was more obstinate, more insistent that they would not fail, that nothing was going to prevent him from achieving his goal. It had taken over their lives and eventually destroyed their marriage.

Lottie pushed the blonde hair away from her face with a hand that shook slightly in the way that the memory of Seraphina always weakened her limbs. She needed to put a stop to this madness now.

She drew in a sharp breath. 'Well, you have wasted this man's time. The idea of us having a baby is totally ridiculous. Why would we even consider it now? After all this time? When our marriage is obviously over?'

Rafael stared across at the wide violet-blue eyes that were searching his face for an explanation. *Certamente*, their marriage was over, all right. It had ended the day Lottie had walked out on him. The day she had told him that she didn't love him. That she had never loved him.

He cursed silently, struggling to keep his frustration inside, rein in the storm of his feelings. He had to remain calm. Not let himself be riled by her fake show of concern or her harsh dismissal of their shared past. He was already a hair's breadth from totally screwing this up, and he knew it.

But what he *hadn't* known was the way his heart would start pounding in his chest the second she walked into the room, as if jolted from a dormant slumber or poked into life by the jab of a stick. What was that? Anger? Betrayal? Lust? Whatever it was, it was damned annoying.

He'd been so sure that the two years they had been apart would have killed any desire he might have had for her. Now he knew that was not the case and he cursed her for it. She had no right to look like that—all heart-shaped face and soft pink lips, her slender body clad in skinny jeans and a plain white shirt, demurely buttoned almost to the top but still failing to conceal the unconscious jut of her breasts as she squared up to him.

Scowling, he raked a hand through his hair.

'Because an accident like this makes you think, Char-

lotte—that's why. Makes you realise that you are not in-
vincible, that you need to plan for the future—a future
when you are no longer around. Ten days in a hospital bed
focusses the mind, believe me, and it gives you plenty of
time to work out what's important.'

'Go on…'

The gentle probing of her voice was threatening to undo
him, unleash a side of him that had nothing to do with the
purpose of this meeting.

'What is important is this place.'

Roughly gesturing around him, he was rewarded with
a sharp stab of pain that shot through his shoulder, mocking him with its power. He would not let it show. Whatever else, Lottie must not see his weakness. He knew she
was watching every movement of his lips, analysing every
syllable of his words. Grimly he carried on.

'The principality is my number one priority. Generations of Revaldis have held the title of Conte di Monterrato. Now it is my turn and I will do everything within my
power to ensure its protection and prosperity.' He paused,
conviction pushing back his shoulders, swelling his chest.
'As you well know, Charlotte, I am the last in line…' he
shot her a piercing stare '…and as such it is my duty to
provide an heir.'

Monterrato. An heir.

Lottie felt the cold fingers of the past reach out to grasp
her. So nothing had changed. It was still all about Monterrato, about providing for its future, continuing the line. The
place was like an obsession with Rafael—everything to
him; his life, his blood. *She* was also the last in line, as it
happened—the sole daughter of John Lamb, deceased, and
Greta Lamb, now Lawrence, remarried and living in South
America. But you didn't hear *her* banging on about it.

'Well, if you are so keen to have a child I suggest you

find someone else to have one with.' Twisting her bottom
on the seat, she sniped back at him, chin high, chest forward. She knew she sounded like a bitter old crow but she
couldn't help herself. 'Judging by the number of women
that seem to constantly surround you, I'm sure you could
have the pick of party socialites only too happy to produce
endless beautiful Monterrato heirs for you.'

Thunder rolled across Rafael's face.

'For God's sake, Charlotte.' His fist banged down on the
desk, rattling the ormolu inkstand on its lion's paws feet.
His eyes were glaring wildly with some unseen force as
they locked with Lottie's, now saucer-shaped with alarm.
'Why can't I make you understand? It is *our* baby I want.'

Lottie's mouth fell open, soft with astonishment. This
was not the calm, composed Rafael that she knew. The man
who was so totally in control of his emotions that she had
never seen him break down—not even when their baby
had died. He was certainly not the kind of man to lose his
temper. At least he never had been.

A thought suddenly occurred to her. He had been in
a terrible accident—an accident that had resulted in injuries to his head. Was it possible that he was suffering
from some sort of post-traumatic mood disorder? Would
that explain the jumpy, volatile, almost out of control man
before her?

'You are right, Rafe, I don't understand.' She lowered
her voice to try and coax the truth out of him. 'Is it something to do with the accident? Has it affected you in some
way?'

The scrape of his chair across the polished parquet floor
made Lottie start as he lunged to his feet, leaning forward
across the desk with the stillness of a viper about to strike.

'Why would you say that?'

'I don't know. I just wondered...' And, judging by his

attitude, she had hit the nail squarely on the head. 'Do you want to talk about it? You never know—it might help.'

Turning his back Rafael strode towards the windows, the floor creaking beneath his forceful steps. 'There is nothing to talk about. It happened. That's all there is to it.' He all but growled the words over his shoulder.

Maledizione. Talking about it was the very last thing he wanted to do. He felt his breath heaving in his chest with the wretched frustration of it all, felt the unfamiliar sense of powerlessness fuelling his temper.

But what had he expected? That Lottie would agree, with no further explanation, to bear him a child just like that?

He could have lied, of course. Wooed her back until he'd achieved his goal, then told her it was all a sham. Just the thought of the challenge heated the blood in his veins. He could feel her eyes scanning his rear view, sense her biting the inside of her cheek as she waited, the rise and fall of her breasts with each shallow breath, the way she slid her hands between tightly pressed thighs as she perched on the edge of her seat. All of which sent hot waves of desire through his body that would make taking her to his bed—hell, taking her across the desk there and then, for that matter—the easiest thing in the world. And who would blame him, after the way she had treated him, if he used her for his own pleasure? But, no, sex wasn't the answer—no matter how tempting it was.

Outside the light was starting to fade, and with the lamps still not lit the room had taken on a grey, almost smoky hue. Lottie feasted her eyes on the proud silhouette, tall, muscular, brooding against the dying light, committing the image to memory before wrenching her gaze away again.

'Well, in that case there is nothing more to be said.'

Her breath juddered and she rose to her feet. 'There is no point in my being here.'

'No! Stop!' Despite his injuries he was beside her in a couple of long strides, grabbing hold of her arm as she reached down to pick up her handbag.

There was a frozen second of astonishment as they stared at each other, then Lottie's eyes moved from the hand that gripped her forearm to the darkening face of the man it belonged to. Instantly dropping her arm, Rafael stepped back, pushing the ruffled hair away from his forehead.

'I'm sorry. Forgive me.'

'Rafe? Whatever is it?'

Throwing back his shoulders, he fixed her with a penetrating stare.

'Okay, Lottie, if you must know I will spell it out for you.'

His voice was harsh, but the anguish and pain held deep in his eyes sent a shiver of alarm through Lottie.

'The fact is that, as of four weeks ago, I am no longer able to father a child. You and our frozen embryo are my only chance of ever producing an heir.'

CHAPTER TWO

'YOU CAN'T EVER have children?' Lottie stared at him, her face a picture of horror.

'Correct.' Rafael remained where he was, his feet firmly planted, his arms behind his back.

'You are…infertile?'

'I think we've established that.' He glowered at her. 'And, before you let your imagination run away with you, that's *all* it means. Everything else is working quite normally, thank you.'

Lottie flushed. He had, of course, read her mind perfectly.

'But why? How?'

'I'll spare you the details, but basically the tree that saved my life prevented me from being able to produce another. A bizarre twist of fate, I think you'll agree.'

The flush turned into an exaggerated wince. Lottie simply didn't know what to say. She could only imagine the devastating effect this must have had on Rafael. Not to mention the physical pain at the time.

'But is it permanent? I mean, won't it heal? Or isn't there some medical procedure that can make it right?'

'It would seem not.' Rafael shifted his position, alerting Lottie to the fact that she was staring at his groin. 'Believe me, I have explored every avenue.'

'Oh, Rafe.' Suddenly Lottie was rushing over to him, flinging her arms around his neck and hugging his unyielding body. 'I'm so sorry.'

Picking her arms from around his rigid neck with a look of distaste, Rafael let them drop by her sides and took a step back. 'It's not your sympathy I am looking for. It is an arrangement of a much more practical kind.'

Lottie gazed up at him, eyes wide with concern.

'I'm *so* sorry,' she repeated, her mind still struggling to take in this shocking disclosure. 'This must be very difficult for you to come to terms with.'

She put a hand out to touch him but he moved out of her reach, crossing his arms in front of him to form a barrier.

'Have you talked this through with anyone? Had any counselling? You mustn't keep it all bottled up inside.'

'Pah!' Rafael gave a derisive snort. 'I do not need counselling, thank you, what I need is a solution to the problem.'

No change there, then; Lottie didn't know why she had even asked the question. She stared at the proud, haughty man who stood stubbornly a few feet away from her. Here was someone who would rather die than give in to his emotions, whose approach to any problem was to get it fixed and move on, rather than take time to grieve or heal.

'Sometimes there is no solution, Rafe. You just have to accept it.'

'Of *course* there is a solution,' he bit back, 'and it lies with you.'

So this was it, then. The reason she was here. Not to sign divorce papers, to end their marriage, but as part of a last desperate attempt by Rafael to provide a Revaldi heir. Lottie bent her head, covering her eyes with her hand as she tried to order her thoughts, formulate some sort of response, explain to him that, no matter how deeply she felt for his predicament, she simply couldn't do it.

'I realise that you hold all the power,' Rafael cut in quickly, hurrying to fill the empty silence before Lottie could say anything negative, 'and that puts me at a disadvantage.'

Power? Disadvantage? Why was he talking like this? As if it were some sort of business merger instead of the birth of a baby, the creation of a new life that should be born of love and commitment and caring. That explained the suit, she thought suddenly. Rafael was simply trying to broker a deal.

'I will agree to your terms, Lottie. Anything. Just say the word and it will be yours.'

'No, Rafe.' She had to stop him now, before this got any worse.

'If it's a question of money...'

Too late. Lottie felt heat rising up her neck, sweeping across her face, as the hideousness of his suggestion took hold.

'Stop it!'

She was starting to shake with a mixture of outrage and sadness—sadness that he could get her so wrong, that he had never understood her at all.

'Do you seriously believe that you can *buy* me? Buy our baby?'

'There's no need to be so melodramatic.' Pushing back his shoulders, he regarded her coldly over the jut of his chin. 'I'm merely trying to find a mutually satisfactory arrangement. Don't tell me you *enjoy* working in that...' he paused, distaste written all over his face '...so-called *art* gallery in London.'

'It's called earning a living.' Lottie glared at him. 'It's what normal people do. And, anyway, how do you know where I work?'

'I made it my business to know.'

'What do you mean by that?' Even as she asked the question the answer hit her like a snowball in the face. 'You have been spying on me?'

'You might call it spying. I call it research. Obviously I had to make sure I had all the available facts at my disposal before I contacted you.'

His calm, rational voice was stoking the fire that was already roaring away inside Lottie.

'There were certain things I needed to ascertain: your career, for example, the state of your finances, whether there was a man in your life.' He shot her a cold, penetrating stare.

Lottie gasped. How *dared* he? And, worse still, how dare he look at her now as if this was perfectly acceptable behaviour? She felt violated, exposed, as if he had stripped away the thin layer of her composure and left her standing naked and shivering in front of him.

'You are telling me that you have hired some private investigator to follow me, lurk in the shadows, pick through my rubbish bins, train his grubby little binoculars on my windows?' The words were tangling around themselves in their hurry to get out and strangle him.

Rafael gave a short laugh. 'Charming though your old-fashioned image is, things have moved on a bit since long macs and trilby hats. The wonders of the internet have taken over.'

'Well, however you did it, it's despicable.' Lottie swept back the hair from her heated face, lifting its weight from the nape of her neck in an attempt to cool herself down. 'You had absolutely no right to go poking about in my life.'

Scowling, Rafael lowered his brows to an aggressive V. 'Needs must, Lottie. Exceptional circumstances call for exceptional measures. Believe me, I wouldn't be doing any of this if there was any other way.'

And that little statement was supposed to make her feel better, was it? If so, then time had clearly not improved Rafael's understanding of the female mind.

Lottie held her glare in place, fearing that, despite her very real anger, her face might easily crumple with the intense sadness of it all. Because of course Rafael wasn't trying to make her feel better, was he? He was just being his usual brutally honest self. Even at a time like this he wasn't able to dress up the situation for his own gain. His nature was to say it as it was and achieve his aim through the sheer power of his conviction.

Quietly she turned away from him, knowing what she had to say but not trusting herself to look into his eyes as she said it. 'I'm sorry, Rafe, but my answer has to be no. We both know that it would never work.'

Instantly Rafael came towards her, repelling her words with a dismissive arm gesture and an expression to match.

'You don't know that.' His voice was hard, uncompromising, as his eyes bore down on her. 'There have been major advances in IVF procedures even in the past couple of years. I'm sure we have every chance...'

'I'm not talking about IVF procedures.' Throwing back her head, Lottie confronted the full force of his gaze. 'I'm talking about us—me and you as a couple. I'm saying that *we* would never work.' The hostility in her voice was there to mask the knot of pain of their failed marriage that sat deep in her stomach, refusing ever to go away.

'Perhaps I am not making myself clear.' Rafael gave her a look of pure disgust, turning his back on her, then swinging round again with eyes that pierced the gloom. 'I'm not asking for any sort of reconciliation. I am asking you solely to be the mother of my child. Nothing more.'

Nothing more? Despite the darkly oppressive atmosphere it was almost laughable, the way he described it—as if he were asking her to redesign his kitchen or landscape his garden. Except that it didn't make her feel like laughing. More like crying.

'What I am trying to say is that I will expect nothing else of you.' Relentlessly, Rafael pushed on. 'I know that that side of our marriage is over. Rest assured I will not be making any…' he paused, firing a look of icy contempt at Lottie '…any *demands* of you.' Distaste soured his mouth, contorted his handsome features. 'You have my word on that.'

Lottie felt something die inside her. She knew it was true, of course, that sexually she was of no interest to him any more. That side of their relationship had floundered after Seraphina had died, bashed against the rocks of invasive fertility treatments and crushing disappointment. But still, hearing him say the words stretched the sadness inside her until she thought she might snap in two, fold over with misery.

But she had to accept it. Rafael had coachloads of women only too happy to cater to his needs now. Flashes of those internet pictures rose, unbidden, in her mind— the dazzling white teeth and pertly sculptured breasts.

She looked down at herself, at the faded skinny jeans she had worn to travel in and her favourite well-worn ankle boots, then switched her gaze to Rafael. There he stood, ramrod-straight before her, that aura of intense concentration almost shimmering around his dark form. The sombre suit was so beautifully cut that you weren't really aware of it—just of the way his body looked in it: powerful, immaculate, sexy. He epitomised everything that she wasn't, and being back at the Palazzo Monterrato only emphasised that fact.

Gathering together the last shreds of her composure, she raised her chin defiantly. 'Thank you for explaining that, Rafael.' Her voice sounded shrill, uneven, like an incompetent schoolteacher trying to keep control of a class. 'Though you really didn't need to point it out. When I said it would never work between us I meant in terms of the practicalities of our relationship.' On firmer ground now, she pressed on determinedly. 'Even supposing I ever did manage to get pregnant, how could we possibly raise a child together? We don't even...' She paused. There were so many *don't evens* that she didn't know which one to pick. 'We don't even live in the same country.'

With the silent step of a panther stalking its prey Rafael closed the space between them, and Lottie suddenly found herself staring at the broad sweep of his chest.

'Practicalities can always be sorted out.'

As he spoke over the top of her head Lottie realised too late that she had chosen a foolish argument. Rafael was the supreme master of being practical, sorting things out. As Conte di Monterrato that was what he did on a daily basis—oversaw the running of the principality, planned for its future, solved the problems. And that was exactly what he was doing now.

So close to him now, Lottie breathed in his familiar scent—the faint tang of cologne mixed with soap and something else, something indefinably, yearningly Rafael. She could almost feel the intensity that emanated from him, rolling her way, threatening to engulf her.

'I don't want you to think for one minute that I am underestimating the enormity of what I am asking of you.' His voice was very low, earnest. 'But at the same time...' his eyes ruthlessly scanned her face '...I don't believe it is an entirely selfish request. I know what being a mother would mean to you.'

Lottie gulped back the lump in her throat, her eyes widening at his startling assumption. 'Why do you say that?'

'Because I saw you, Lottie.' His pause shimmered with raw emotion. 'I saw the look of euphoria on your face when we found out that you were pregnant—saw the way your maternal instinct kicked in, stronger than any other bond. And then...' He carried on, even though he looked as if he was hurting inside. 'I saw the way you held our daughter in your arms.'

'No. Stop!' This was more than Lottie could bear and her hands flew to cover her ears.

'Admit it, Lottie. It was never me that you wanted, was it?' Relentlessly he surged on. 'It was the baby. The baby was the only thing that mattered. The only reason you ever agreed to marry me. And our marriage was nothing more than a sham. Your final brutal declaration—everything about your behaviour, in fact—points to that one undeniable truth.'

'I won't listen to this any more!' Turning away, Lottie stumbled towards the door, but he was still there—following her, beside her.

'You can still have that dream, Lottie. Even though our marriage may be over in all but name we can still be parents—you can still be that mother.'

'I have no idea why you are saying this.' Blinking back the emotion that was stinging her eyes, Lottie rounded on him, drawing on every last bit of strength she possessed. 'I can only assume you are confusing this with what *you* want, not me.'

'Maybe I thought that too at first.' Rafael positioned himself in front of the door, his towering shape blocking Lottie's exit. 'Until I saw the look on your face just now. I'm right, aren't I? You want a baby every bit as much as I do.'

'No, you are *not* right.' Futilely trying to move him out

of the way, Lottie grabbed hold of the door handle and tugged at it forcefully.

The door opened two inches before it slammed against Rafael.

'Be careful what you decide, Lottie.' He looked down at her calmly, totally ignoring the door battering against his heels as she continued to tug at it. 'Whatever you do, don't let your contempt for me influence your decision— get in the way of your own happiness.'

Finally he moved to one side and the door flew open, sending Lottie teetering off balance.

'That would never do.'

Kicking off her boots, Lottie threw herself down on to the four-poster bed and stared at the tapestry drapes above her, her breath heaving unsteadily in her chest, tears now threatening to spill. How could he do this to her? Taunt her with her failed attempt at motherhood using the preciously painful memories of Seraphina. It was simply cruel.

But that was Rafael. She knew he would stop at nothing to achieve his goal—use anything at his disposal to get what he wanted. Even if it meant tearing open her heart in the process.

Like a double-edged sword, the pain cut both ways, and one slash undoubtedly revealed the truth. She *had* always wanted to be a mother. Not in the vague, one day it would be nice, mentally picking out cute names way that her girlfriends seemed to view motherhood, but with a deep, unfathomable yearning that was intrinsically a part of who she was.

Maybe her own dysfunctional upbringing had made her realise that being a mother was the most important job of all and, rather than putting her off having children, had instilled in her a longing do it right. There was no doubt that when she had discovered she was pregnant with Rafael's baby it had flooded her with euphoric exhilaration. This was her chance to be the sort of mother she had always wanted, rather than the one she had had.

As the only child of a woman who, frankly, had had better things to do than pander to the whims of an annoyingly childlike child, Lottie had been largely raised by au pairs or home helps or whatever neighbour happened to be around. This had left Greta free to indulge in her real passion: travelling. Or, more specifically, cruising the world on luxury liners while Lottie had lived in a perpetual state of terror that one day there would be nobody to meet her at the school gates at all.

Funded by Lottie's much older father, who had thoughtfully taken out a comprehensive life insurance policy before he'd dropped dead when Lottie was still only seven, Greta had become addicted to the glamour of the cruising lifestyle: the handsome stewards in their crisp white uniforms, the perma-tanned dance hosts, the dashing captains. Eventually she had ended up in dry dock with one of the latter, when she had remarried and made a new life in Argentina.

But the other slash of Rafael's sword... Lottie screwed up her eyes against its searing pain, at the realisation that he'd got it so wrong. *'It was never me that you wanted... The baby was the only thing that mattered.'* Was it possible that he actually believed that? That she had really done such a good job of fooling him? And, if so, why did it make her feel so hollowed out with sadness?

Taking a deep breath, she pushed herself up against the feather pillows and gazed at the room around her. It was the same bedroom she had shared with Rafael—well, half of it, at any rate. The huge double doors across the middle of the room were now firmly closed, like a metaphor for their marriage.

How different would things have been if they hadn't lost Seraphina? If there had been no accident? If everything hadn't gone so disastrously wrong? Their daughter would have been three now, running around this crusty old mausoleum, breathing fresh life into it, maybe even joined by a little brother or sister.

But it had happened, and the sequence of events afterwards had happened, leading to her going back to England, starting a new life in London and putting the past behind her. Even if that new life *had* meant studiously avoiding babies of all descriptions—babies in buggies, baby adverts on the television—and even turning away from babies smiling gummily at her over their mothers' shoulders on the bus.

But she had never lost her yearning to have a baby, Rafael's baby. And she had never forgotten their last remaining embryo. The tiny blob of shared cells stored in a tank of liquid nitrogen represented the last vestiges of their relationship and it was always there, locked away deep in her subconscious. Occasionally she would find herself fantasising about the sort of child it might grow into, before hurriedly pushing the thought back in its box and turning the key once more.

And now...now the embryo was being offered its chance of life. Never in her wildest dreams had she imagined that circumstances would bring about a possibility like this. It was a mad, crazy, ridiculous idea.

Wasn't it?

Rafael paced up and down the length of the grand formal dining room, pausing only to check his watch once again. Where the hell *was* she? She knew that dinner was to be served at eight-thirty and she was now an hour late. Was she deliberately taunting him?

It was half an hour since he had gone up to find her, when the sudden, irrational fear had gripped him. He'd pounded his feet along the corridor to her room, convinced that she had gone—run away as she had before. He'd rapped sharply on the door, and the thirty seconds of silence before he had heard her moving about had seemed like an eternity.

But then the door had opened and there she'd been—all sleepy eyes and tousled hair, straight from a rumpled bed still warm from her body. And the sight of her, and that bed, had twisted a coil of lust deep inside of him.

Now that she still hadn't appeared he could feel the same fear spreading through him again. Ten minutes, she had said—just enough time for a quick shower. Pacing back towards the head of the table, he told himself to calm down, get a grip. Stop behaving like an idiot.

He was glaring at the heavy panelled door when it finally opened and Lottie hurried in, all breathless apologies and pointed lack of eye contact. Reaching behind him for the bell that rang down in the kitchens, he waited in cold silence as she walked the interminable length of the table to join him. He watched from beneath the sweep of lowered lashes as she carefully sat down, sliding long legs under the table, shaking open her napkin to cover her lap.

Tearing his eyes away, he seated himself beside her at the head of the table, steadfastly refusing to acknowledge just how adorable she looked. Her hastily washed and dried hair had resulted in a cloud of tumbling blonde curls that she had loosely twisted into a knot on top of her head, and already escaping tendrils were framing her delicate features. A short jersey dress, its colour a darkest purple, hugged her slender curves in a way that already had the blood racing around his veins.

Lifting a heavy crystal decanter, he started to fill Lottie's glass, watching as her slender fingers curled nervously around the stem. Then, raising his own glass between them, he saw Lottie automatically doing the same. What exactly were they toasting? With her meltingly clear blue eyes mercilessly trained on him he felt for the bedrock of bitterness to help him counter their effect and found it in the pit of his stomach, where it had sat ever since she had left him.

'Your good health.'

It was hardly the warmest of toasts. Lottie looked at his darkly glowering face over the rim of her wine glass. She knew he was angry that she was late for dinner; he had already been in a bad mood when he had woken her up from her unexpected nap, banging on her bedroom door, demanding to know what was keeping her. But her promise of ten minutes had proved impossible to achieve and, torn between nervousness at keeping him waiting and a desire to make herself look at least half decent, the latter had won.

Though now she wondered why she had bothered. It would appear that her hastily applied makeover had simply darkened Rafael's already coal-black mood.

'Yes—*salute*.' After taking a small sip, Lottie put down her glass and concentrated on straightening the already straight silver cutlery, wondering just how she was going to get through this ordeal.

Almost immediately two waiting staff appeared, and in the flurry of dishes being revealed from under domed silver lids and food being expertly served onto their plates Lottie was able to ignore, at least for the moment, the ill-tempered man at her side.

When the staff finally left he pointedly waited for her to pick up her knife and fork before doing the same.

'I suggest we eat this now, before it is completely ruined.'

He really was determined to be relentlessly bad-tempered, wasn't he? This evening was going to be horrendous.

But the meal was delicious and, seated beside Rafael in this magnificent cavernous room, drinking mellow red wine from the ancient, vaulted cellars beneath them, Lottie could feel herself being transported back to the life of wealth and privilege that she had torn herself away from so violently two long years ago. Rafael's world. And even though he was casually dressed now, in jeans and a soft cotton shirt open at the collar, he still looked every inch the master—every inch the Conte di Monterrato.

The conversation was limited, with Lottie's attempt at small talk falling on stony ground and Rafael seemingly too intent on eating his meal to discuss the weightier subject, though it hovered between them like an uninvited guest at the meal.

Instead Lottie found herself surreptitiously watching him, drawn to the shape of his mouth as it moved, the sweeping line of his jaw, now shadowed with a stubble that covered some of the bruising, the way dark curls fell over his forehead when he lowered his head, only to be pushed back with an impatient hand. In the flickering light of the candelabra set on the table between them his injuries were much less visible, and he looked alarmingly like the old, impossibly handsome Rafael.

The meal finally over, Rafael suggested that they go into the salon and, reluctantly relinquishing her hold on a crumpled linen napkin, Lottie followed him across the marble hallway into the warmth of the relatively modest room. Coffee and cognac were waiting for them on a low table in front of the fire and they seated themselves side by side on the antique sofa. Rafael started to pour her a balloon glass of brandy but Lottie shook her head. She had had enough alcohol; she could feel it seeping into her bones, threatening to muddle her senses. Coffee was a much more sensible idea.

Wrestling with the heavy silver pot, she poured coffee into two china cups and passed one to Rafael. Then crossing her legs, she tried to settle herself beside him, one hand holding a rattling cup, the other one tugging her dress down over her thighs.

'So, have you thought any more about my suggestion?'

The truce was obviously over, and the air was immediately filled with the magnitude of his question.

'Of course I have.' She turned to face him, the sofa springs twanging beneath her. 'And I must say that I don't appreciate the emotional blackmail.'

Rafael spanned the fingers of one hand across his temples, shielding his eyes as if it pained him even to look at her. 'I was merely pointing out that you have a strong maternal instinct. There is no need to be ashamed about that.'

'I'm not ashamed!'

'So you are not denying, then, that in theory you would like to have a baby?' Suddenly he was giving her the full force of his gaze again.

'Yes…no. That is not the point.'

'Because if you would, Lottie, now is your chance to do something about it. I'm sure I don't need to tell you that with the fertility problems you have suffered your chances of having a child with someone else might well prove…challenging.'

'And yours would be non-existent.'

It was a cruel jibe and Lottie could feel the heat of it slash across her cheeks. But she wasn't going to take it back; he deserved it.

'*Touché.*'

He owned the few dark seconds of silence and Lottie felt increasingly bad with each one that passed.

'So we are both in the same situation. And that has to be all the more reason to make the right decision now.'

Lottie placed her cup back down on the table. He had an answer for everything, didn't he? Except Seraphina. He never wanted to talk about their baby daughter. Well, now she was going to make him.

She sucked in a deep, empowering breath. 'Do you ever think about Seraphina?' The out-breath of words whistled between them like a bullet. And she knew her aim had been sure by the immediate clench of Rafael's jaw.

'Of course I do.' His voice was sharp but he still couldn't hide the emotion behind it. Neither could the shuttered look in his eyes that were fixed on her face. 'How can you even ask such a question? Seraphina was my baby too, in case you've forgotten.'

The vulnerability had gone, immediately replaced with the more familiar animosity, but she had caught a glimpse of it—heard him say her name. *Seraphina.* Spoken with that beautiful Italian intonation. It was all she could do not to ask him to repeat it, over and over again, until she was full to the brim with it.

She looked down from his injured face to the hand that was resting on his muscular thigh, the back of it criss-crossed with the scars and scratches from his accident, reminding her yet again just what he had been through.

Impulse made her reach towards it, tentatively rest her own pale hand over the top of it. 'Maybe I have. I'm sorry.'

The connection between them was immediate, tingling with the sharp pinpricks of recalled intimacy, until Rafael quickly pulled away, running the same hand through his hair as if to cleanse himself of her. He moved slightly in his seat as he took control again.

'I know we can never replace Seraphina, nor would we

want to, but there is nothing to stop us having a healthy child, Lottie. I want you to understand that.'

'Rafe...'

'Just imagine, Lottie...a year from now we could be parents. We can make this happen—I know we can.'

'You don't know that.' Trying to hang on to the last vestiges of sanity, Lottie challenged him. 'Even if I agreed to the embryo transplantation there is nothing to say that it will work.'

'But there is one certainty.' His commanding voice was very low. 'If we don't try we will never know.'

Suddenly the room was stiflingly hot, its silence only broken by the hiss and rustle of the logs settling down on the fire. With the intensity of Rafael's dark eyes boring into her Lottie felt the heat sweep through her body, softening her bones, melting away the layers of resolve that had settled comfortably over her like a blanket of snow.

Could she say yes? Rafael somehow made the decision sound so straightforward. He made everything seem possible. But then he had no thought or care for the life she had made for herself in England. Built up so painstakingly, brick by brick, from the demolition rubble of their marriage. She had finally reached the stage where she felt financially stable and emotionally settled. Most of the time anyway.

Could she really take this enormous gamble and throw caution, common sense and self-preservation to the wind? Hurl them up into the blue sky and watch to see where they fell? The same blue sky that Rafael had fallen from, that had brought her here in the first place.

It was so tempting.

Rafael waited, as if sensing that words were no longer needed. So close now she could feel the soft whisper of his breath against her face, feel herself weakening beneath the unbearable scrutiny of his gaze and the lethal, sensual intoxication of his nearness.

Sitting up very straight, she pushed back her shoulders and mirrored his penetrating stare. This was her decision and she was going to make it.

'Right, I have made up my mind.'

The answering flash in Rafael's eyes was so intense that she had to blink against it, her mouth suddenly dry with the cotton wool words.

'My answer is yes. I will do it.'

CHAPTER THREE

THERE WAS A long second of astonishment. Then, jerking back to life, Rafael clasped Lottie's hands in his, squeezing them tightly in his strong grasp.

'You mean it?' He angled his head to see her face better, to make sure he had understood correctly.

'Yes.'

'You agree to using our frozen embryo?'

'Yes. That *is* what we are talking about here, isn't it?' She attempted a short laugh but it came out as more of a squawk, the panic of what she had just agreed to throttling her vocal cords.

'Then I thank you.' Deeply serious now, Rafael let go of her hands and, tipping her chin with his fingers, captured her gaze with his own. *'Vi ringrazio dal profondo del mio cuore.* Thank you from the bottom of my heart.'

'That's okay.'

Lottie cringed at her vapid reply. *Okay* was hardly a fitting response to Rafael's heartfelt gratitude. Or to the magnitude of what she had agreed to, come to that. But she couldn't think straight—not when he was so close, not when he was looking at her like that, with the soft touch of his fingertips searing against her skin. She needed to get away—away from Rafael and the way he was making her feel. If she had just made the most crazy decision of her life she wanted to be alone now, so that she could scream at herself in peace.

'Well, I think I'll go to bed.' She wobbled to standing. 'I am rather tired.'

'Of course.' Rafael was immediately beside her, holding her elbow. 'We can discuss all the arrangements tomorrow.'

That little statement did nothing to calm her nerves. She went to move away but Rafael held on to her, drawing her closer, his strong arms encircling her body, pressing her against his chest. Lottie froze beneath his embrace.

'You won't regret this decision, Lottie.'

She could feel his breath fanning the top of her head, lightly moving her hair.

'I will make sure of that. This time it will work—I know it will.'

'I hope so.' Her words were muffled against the soft cotton of his shirt.

She had no idea whether it would or not, but right now she had a more pressing concern—literally. The shocking way her body was reacting to his. The initial forbidden twitch of desire had spread through her body, stopping somewhere low in her abdomen, where it now sat, throbbing inside her, waiting for something to happen.

'I know so.'

He pulled her even closer and Lottie felt any resolve fade away as the heat between them intensified. It felt so good, yet so wrong, encased in his muscular arms, with the hard planes of his chest crushing her breasts against him with alarming effect, the lengths of their bodies touching, meeting all the way down.

Ignoring every screaming warning, she found herself arching her body very slightly, to push her pelvis closer to him, to feel more. And she wasn't disappointed. The rock-hard length of his arousal was instantly evident, making its presence felt against her, and her own body immediately went into clenching spasms of desire in response. A thrill of triumph rushed through her that she could still do this to him—that he wasn't as impervious to her as his icy façade would suggest. Up on tiptoes now, she tentatively moved her arms around his neck, wanting more, for *him* to want more.

She heard the guttural growl, followed by a soft Italian curse, then felt her arms being wrenched from his neck, left to fall by her sides as he jerked himself away from her.

'No!'

The word was like a lash-stroke across the exposed flesh of Lottie's desire.

'That is *not* what this is about.'

Standing alone, rejected and exposed, Lottie could only stare at him, watching with wide-eyed confusion as he strode over to the fireplace, kicking a stray log back into the hearth with a shower of sparks.

'I think we need to lay down some ground rules.' He barked the words over his shoulder at her. 'I don't want you getting the wrong idea.'

The wrong idea.

Lottie pulled her gaze from the rigid tension of his back to the empty space where he had stood. Her body was still twitching with desire, her legs trembling beneath her. But his words had shrivelled her heart. We wouldn't want Lottie getting *the wrong idea*, would we? As if he might actually have any *feelings* for her.

Pushing the hair away from her face, she straightened her dress and cleared her throat. She needed to take control now—convince him that she wasn't bothered, that he was overreacting.

'That's okay.' She attempted a throwaway laugh. 'It was nothing. There's no need to get all heavy about it.'

Rafael spun round and gave her a look that bordered on hatred. Swallowing back the bile, he planted his feet firmly apart, glaring at her. '*Si, certo*. Nothing.'

Lottie bit down on her trembling lip. Well, what did he *want* her to say, for God's sake? She was trying to make this better. The shameless way she had wanted him, the humiliation of being abandoned, the look of pure disgust on Rafael's face now—all conspired to make her feel suitably wretched. Now she had to put up some form of defence.

'What I mean is I am fully aware of the situation.' Her voice was surprisingly cold, clear. 'I have agreed to try for this baby with you, Rafael, not to resurrect our marriage.'

Rafael swung round to face her, thunder in his eyes. 'As long as we both know where we stand.'

'I'm sure we do. You have made your feelings towards me perfectly clear.'

'And yours towards me.'

'Yes.'

Lottie flinched. Her big black lie. Impossible to remove now. It was stitched into the fabric of Rafael's being. It was there in every twitch of his muscles, every hitch of his shoulders, every coal-black stare of his eyes.

With a couple of strides he was before her again, glowering down on her defensive body. Lottie faced the wall of his hostility, watching him struggle to control his breathing, his temper, his dislike of her. Struggling with all the things he would not say.

Finally he stepped back, his eyes refusing to leave her face.

'Then I am glad there is no confusion.'

Rafael drained his brandy glass and banged it down on the coffee table in front of him, the emotional roller coaster ride of the evening still wreaking havoc on his body. He ran a hand over his forehead, the ridge of his scar a timely reminder of the accident that had started all this.

He should have been feeling elated. If nothing else he had managed to persuade Lottie to agree to using their frozen embryo. Now he needed to get things moving before she changed her mind—or, worse still, went back to England, met someone else, forgot all about him. He had been fortunate, he had to concede, that that hadn't already happened. That she hadn't already taken up with some uncomplicated young man and started living a happily-ever-after that certainly didn't include him. But his investigations had revealed nothing apart from that slimeball of a boss at the gallery where she worked.

He flexed his fingers. *There* was a guy asking for a punch on the nose if ever there was one. But even if she was unattached now he had had no way of telling for how long. He'd had to act fast.

But not in the way he just had. *Dio...* His hand came down over his eyes. What the hell had he been thinking of, pressing himself up against her like a horny teenager? Displaying, oh, so physically, just how easily she could still turn him on? Because she did, didn't she? Every little *male-detto* thing about her sent his logical brain into a tailspin south. And to the trouble that was waiting for him there.

Though it hadn't just been him. The memory of the way Lottie had responded still pulsed through his veins. Had that been deliberate? A test to see what it would take to make him react? If so, he had shown himself to be the weakest of creatures. She had eventually swept from the room, seemingly not able to get away from him fast enough, presumably gloating with the satisfaction that she could turn him on just like that, just the way she always had.

Well, *enough*. Getting up from the sofa, he stretched

back his shoulders, circling them up and around to ease the stiffness, almost enjoying the physical pain that shot down one side of his body. He had to resist, be strong. Moving over to the fireplace, he caught sight of his battered reflection in the enormous gilt mirror, demonstrating yet again the mess he had made of his life. He looked away quickly, only to be confronted by the carved marble cherubs on either side of him, mocking him with their adoring faces.

Sometimes it felt as if the whole world had it in for him.

The next morning dawned bright and clear and Lottie witnessed every stage of it. After a few fitful hours of sleep she had given up and spent what was left of the night huddled on the window seat, her duvet pulled around her. There she had watched the starlit night giving way to the first flush of pink, the curved sliver of the sun making its miraculous appearance, rising with surprising speed until it hung above its unmade bed, ready for the day.

Those silent hours had given her plenty of time to go over everything—over and over, until she had thought her head would burst with it. But now, up and dressed, warmed by the coffee from her otherwise untouched breakfast tray, she found her mind was surprisingly clear and she knew what she had to do.

Pulling her phone out of her bag, she first texted her friend and flatmate Alex, spelling out that she planned to stay at Monterrato 'for a few weeks more'. There was no way Alex would be up yet, so at least she was excused having to speak to her and face the barrage of questions that this breezily worded statement would no doubt produce.

Pressing 'send', she couldn't help but smile at the thought of Alex's reaction, already envisaging her colourfully worded reply.

The next one was more difficult. Informing Ibrahim,

her boss at the gallery, that the 'three or four days' she had taken off work to come here might actually now be more like three or four weeks was not going to go down well. He was prone to bouts of hysteria at the best of times and this was undoubtedly going to ramp up his rage levels. Still, it had to be done. So, punching his number into the phone, Lottie tucked her hair behind her ear, cleared her throat and waited for the soothing buzzing of the connection tone to be shattered by his familiar bark.

The *palazzo* was quiet and still when Lottie finally stepped out onto the landing, the air smelling of polish and freshly cut flowers. Descending the stairs, she looked cautiously around her, feeling the smooth mahogany banister run beneath her hand. She crossed the hall and, pulling open the heavy studded front door, took in a deep, restorative breath.

The Monterrato estate spread out in all directions, as far as the eye could see, sparkling with early-morning dew. In front of her stretched two rows of towering poplar trees, casting strong diagonal shadows across the long driveway that cut through the manicured lawns on either side.

Lottie descended one of the twin flights of stairs and crunched along the gravel path that followed the side of the *palazzo*. The crisp, cold air felt good against her cheeks and she breathed it in greedily, feeling it scour the insides of her body.

With her hands pushed deep inside her coat pockets she strode purposefully on, knowing exactly where she was going—past the kitchen gardens and the outbuildings, the deserted stables and the swimming pool, to a winding path that threaded through a wooded area.

The first signs of spring were starting to appear: snow-drops and crocus were defiantly poking their heads through the cold soil, scattered around the feet of the trees. The path gradually ascended until the trees stopped and there, perched on the top of a hill, was the Monterrato chapel, its burnt umber walls stark against the pearly blue morning sky.

A shallow flight of stone steps, overgrown with moss and weeds, led up to the chapel and the graves that were spread out around it, their headstones tipping drunkenly in the cold sunshine. This was the final resting place for generations of Revaldis, at peace in these beautiful surroundings.

Lottie moved respectfully between them, picking a pathway towards one particular very small grave. The sight of it clutched at her heart. There was the carved angel, still faithfully guarding the slab of painfully clean white marble, one cheek resting on her hands, her wings spread out behind her.

Squatting down, Lottie took a moment to steady herself as the memories came flooding back: the sight of the tiny white coffin being lowered into the ground, the sound of the first handful of soil as it had landed on the lid. Reaching forward, she touched the headstone, her cold fingers tracing the inscription, the words carved into her heart.

Someone had placed a posy of fresh flowers in a small urn and as she absently rearranged them a robin perched on the angel's head, watching her with its beady eyes. All was peaceful and still. Savouring the precious moment, Lottie uttered a small, silent prayer to her daughter and watched as the robin took off, carrying her blessings up into the sky.

'Lottie?'

Lottie swung round with a start. Rafael was standing a few yards away, tall and dark in a long black overcoat, the raised collar skimming his bruised jawline, like some dashing Victorian villain.

'I thought I might find you here.'

Stumbling to her feet, Lottie pulled her coat closer to her. 'I…I just needed to think—to be with Seraphina.'

'Of course. You don't need to explain. I will go…leave you in peace.' He was already turning away.

'No.' Suddenly she knew she didn't want him to go. She wanted him to stand with her, beside their daughter's grave, together. Not to distance himself in the way he always had. 'Why don't you join us?'

If the words sounded flippant they both knew the very real intent that they held. Lottie watched as Rafael hesitated, wariness, uncertainty and pride crossing his face before he quietly moved between the overgrown graves to join her, standing sentry-tall beside the towering angel.

There was a short moment of painfully poignant silence, abruptly ended when Rafael shifted his position and gave a small cough.

'You look cold, Lottie. We should go back to the *palazzo*. There are things we need to discuss.'

'I'm fine.' A shiver so violent that it shook her shoulders said otherwise.

Registering the challenge in her voice, he increased the authority of his own. 'Then come into the chapel. It will be warmer in there.'

There was no point in arguing. Lottie followed him to the arched doorway of the chapel and watched as he turned the heavy iron ring on the door.

The small space welcomed them in with its domed sky-blue ceiling, sprinkled with hundreds of gold stars and the gilded altar at the back watched over by the Madonna and child. There was that particular, evocative smell—a mixture of wood and damp and incense.

Walking between the rows of ancient pews, Rafael went to light a candle at the altar, then joined Lottie on the front pew, his long legs stretched before him. They were quiet for a moment, neither wanting to break the spell.

'So...' Eventually Rafael spoke, his voice low and respectful of their environment. 'Your decision last night...'

He turned guardedly to face her, and Lottie noticed that the cold had puckered his scar to a white slash.

'...it still stands?'

'Yes, of course.' She returned his look defiantly.

'Good.' He let out a breath that lowered his shoulders. 'Then I thank you again. I'm sure I don't need to tell you how much this means to me.'

'No, you don't Rafael.' Lottie clasped her cold hands together. 'And, despite the novelty, please don't think that you have to keep thanking me either.'

'As you wish.' He looked at her curiously, trying to gauge her mood. 'Perhaps you would prefer me to move on to the practicalities?'

Lottie wouldn't prefer it, as it happened, but she knew that she had no choice. She scuffed her feet against the ancient tiles.

'Dr Oveisi will be arriving at two-thirty tomorrow.'

'What?' That stopped the breath in her throat.

'Yes. We were fortunate. He had a free day.'

Of course he had. World-renowned IVF specialists were bound to have plenty of time on their hands—empty diaries just waiting for a call. At least that was how it always seemed to work in Rafael's world.

'Tomorrow.' She repeated the word slowly, trying to get it to sink in.

She didn't know why she was surprised. Rafael was a man who, once a decision had been made, acted on it there and then. He was hardly going to suggest a cooling off period—thirty days in which she could change her mind, cancel her contract.

And, despite the shot of panic she had to concede that there was no point in delaying things. She wasn't going to change her mind. The sooner they did this, the sooner they would know if it had worked. And if it did...? Just the thought of that sent a giddy thrill of excitement all the way down to her wriggling toes.

Yesterday, when she had made her decision, it had almost felt as if someone else had taken over her body. Some reckless, feckless madam who had elbowed her sensible self to one side, gagged her with a frivolously decadent undergarment and said, *Yes, Rafael, of course I will agree to this preposterous idea.*

She had strongly suspected that the morning would see her deeply regretting the idea. But her sleepless night had produced more than the dark circles under her eyes. Those chilly hours of darkness had focussed her mind, made her see things more clearly than ever before. She had realised that Rafael was right; she *did* want to be a mother and, even though she hated to admit it even to herself, more than anything in the world she wanted to be the mother of Rafael's child.

This was her one opportunity to make it happen—the embryo's one chance of life. To say no now would be closing the door on that dream for ever, effectively agreeing that their embryo should be destroyed. Something she knew she could never, ever do. Today she was surprised to find that she felt strong—empowered, even, by her decision. This was a huge, massive risk she was taking, but what was it that people said? That life's biggest regrets came not from the things you had done but the things you hadn't? Well, she wasn't going to be accused of that—not this time. No way.

Gazing around the chapel, she felt a flutter of anticipation go through her. If their future chance of parenthood was now in the lap of the gods this felt like the right place to be: seated next to Rafael in this timeless capsule of calm, with the Madonna and child before them. She took strength from that.

'Tomorrow is all right with you?'

Rafael's question cut through Lottie's thoughts and she realised he was waiting for her reply.

'I thought we might as well move this on as fast as we can.'

'Tomorrow is fine.' She turned to face him full-on, even risking a bright-eyed smile. 'The sooner we can do this the better.'

Dr Oveisi turned out to be a rather dapper, middle-aged man with blue-black slicked-back hair and a fondness for gold jewellery. As Lottie nervously shook his outstretched hand she could feel the chunky rings against her sweaty palm.

They were seated in the grand salon—Lottie and Rafael side by side on the sofa, Dr Oveisi on a high-backed chair opposite. It soon became apparent that he was both highly intelligent and not a man to mess around. Rafael's kind of man. After the briefest of introductions he launched straight into questions about Lottie's fertility history, the failed IVF attempts and her current ovulation cycle.

All the while his fountain pen scratched over the notepad he held on his lap, making indecipherable black marks. But for all his lack of social skills Lottie quickly found herself trusting him. There was no schmoozing, no small talk—here was a man in the business of making babies, and everything about him said that was exactly what he intended to do for them.

Beside her Rafael sat quietly, listening intently. Lottie could sense his concentration, the significance of the conversation only really evident in the stiff posture of his body.

Moving on from Lottie's fertility deficiencies, Dr Oveisi turned his attention to the precious embryo. More notes were taken as Rafael confirmed that, yes, it had been frozen at five days old, and gave the name of the fertility clinic where it was stored.

'And there is only *one* blastocyst?' Looking up briefly, Dr Oveisi directed the question at Rafael.

They both knew the term blastocyst: an embryo that had been cultured for five days. Three gruelling rounds of IVF had left them horribly familiar with all the medical terminology.

'Yes.' The lack of emotion in Rafael's clipped reply was telling. 'Just the one.'

'Right.' Screwing the top back on his fountain pen and stowing it in his inside pocket, Dr Oveisi stood up. 'I think that is everything. I will arrange a visit from one of our fertility nurses to discuss Contessa Revaldi's hormone injections. Once we have a date for the transfer I will see you at the clinic.'

Allowing himself the smallest of smiles, he held out his hand to shake Lottie's, bowing slightly before leaving the room with Rafael.

Lottie found herself gazing at his vacated seat. This was all happening so fast. Dr Oveisi, for all his brusque impersonality, had made it seem real, tangible. Was it really possible that a few weeks from now she could be pregnant? Pregnant with Rafael's child?

As promised, the fertility nurse turned up the next day, carrying her bag full of potions. Lottie immediately liked her—a young Eastern European called Gina, obviously very bright, and attractive with it. Her crisp white uniform set off her slender figure nicely, her hair was scraped back into a bouncy ponytail and her intelligent blue eyes held a steady gaze.

Until she saw Rafael, of course. Lottie could almost see her trying to control the *phwoar!* response, fighting to remain professional in the face of this alarmingly handsome man.

Rafael treated her to a polite smile before announcing that he would leave them to it. Alone together, the two women exchanged a glance, and the flush on Gina's face took its time to recede as she turned away to open her bag, fumbling inside for her equipment.

Gina had intended to come and administer the hormone injections every day, until Lottie told her that she could do it for herself. It wasn't as if she hadn't done it before. She watched as Lottie pushed her first injection into her thigh and, obviously satisfied that she knew what she was doing, left her with instructions on the strict routine she had to follow until her next visit.

'And I don't need to tell you about the possible side effects either?' Gina gave Lottie a sympathetic smile.

'Headaches, stomach cramps, mood swings, hot flushes... Looking forward to it already.' Lottie grinned back. 'Been there—got the tee shirt.'

'Well, I hope it's a baggy one,' Gina replied. 'You'll need it to cover the baby bump!'

'Let's hope so.'

The two women looked at each other.

'This *is* Dr Oveisi we are talking about here,' said Gina. 'He takes hope and turns it into reality.'

Gina's faith was touching, even if it did sound a little like a line from a fertility clinic brochure.

Gazing at the array of medication spread out on the table

in front of her forcefully brought home to Lottie what she had to go through—what she had agreed to do. But there was no going back now.

'Yes, I promise I will tell you all about it when I get back. Yes… No… I'm fine. Honestly, Alex, there's nothing for you to worry about. Now, you get back to your Pinot Grigio and let me get some sleep. It's gone midnight here, I'll have you know.'

Lottie ended the call and twisted round to put her phone down on the bedside table. She loved Alex, she really did, but she was becoming increasingly difficult to fob off—especially after a glass or two of wine fuelled her slightly slurred determination to find out, *'Just what is going on over there, Lots?'*

Lottie had lived the past few days in a bubble of unreality—the situation being so crazy that she could hardly come to terms with it herself, let alone try to explain it to someone as excitable as Alex.

She had arrived at Monterrato convinced that she would be signing divorce papers, severing all ties with Rafael, and yet now here she was, trying to get pregnant with his baby and wanting it more desperately than she dared admit even to herself.

Turning out the light, she curled up under the duvet. Her life back in England seemed very far away right now, even though she knew she was going to have to face up to it again at some point—especially the small matter of her job at the Ibrahim Gallery. Ibrahim himself had made it quite clear that he would not authorise any extended leave and that if she wasn't back at her desk within the week there would be no desk for her to come back to. Bearing in mind that threat, she was now left wondering whether she actually had a job at all.

Meanwhile her time at the *palazzo* had settled into a bizarre pattern. Business took Rafael away a lot, and even when he was there Lottie saw very little of him. If he wasn't buried in his office he was chairing meetings in the boardroom, or out and about somewhere in the principality, dealing with the many and complex issues that being the Conte di Monterrato involved.

When their paths did cross he would politely enquire after her well-being. It felt genuine enough, even if he was just checking up on her—checking that she was following Dr Oveisi's instructions to the letter. But something about the way he'd glance at his wristwatch or feel in his pocket for his phone made it quite clear that he had no intention of prolonging their conversations.

It felt almost as if Lottie was just another of the many projects he was dealing with, but even though it still hurt his cool disregard didn't fool her for one moment. She knew this was typical Rafael Revaldi behaviour. That the more something meant to him the less he would let it show.

It was the nights that were the worst—especially when she knew Rafael was around. The thought of him so close, asleep in his bed just the other side of those dividing doors but so far removed from her emotionally, filled her with a yearning sadness. She realised that she had never felt more alone.

Now, as she lay very still, she could hear sounds from next door. Straining her ears, she listened to the creak of Rafael's footsteps on the wooden flooring, the faint hum of the shower. With her imagination intent on torturing her she pictured the low-slung towel around his hips, the damp-slicked hair on his chest and forearms, his biceps bunching as he roughly dried his hair...

Hearing the creak of the bed, she knew that the towel

had now been dropped to the floor and he was sliding, muscular and naked, between the cool linen sheets...

Finally the day of the embryo transfer arrived. It had been arranged that Lottie would drive herself to the clinic and Rafael, who had been in Paris for the past few days, would meet her there.

It was about a two-hour journey, but Lottie knew the way well enough. It was the same clinic where she had undergone the treatments before—where their last remaining precious embryo was stored. But somehow this time, with Dr Oveisi in charge, everything felt different.

As the countryside flew by Lottie settled into the journey. She loved driving this car—one of the fleet of vehicles that Rafael owned. It was a sleek black beast that ate up the miles with silent ease. And it was a relief to finally get away from the *palazzo*—away from the inquisitive eyes of the staff.

She knew they had to be curious about what was going on between the Conte and his bolter of a wife. She would have been, in their shoes. If it was a reconciliation it was a most peculiar one. Half the time Rafael wasn't around, and the other half he kept her at a distance so respectful it bordered on frigid. Hardly the behaviour of a reunited pair of lovebirds.

But with each advancing mile Lottie felt her nerves increasing. The radio was no distraction either. The jangly love songs seemed deliberately to highlight the absurdity of her situation. Slowing down a little, she felt for a bottle of water and gulped down several mouthfuls.

What she was about to do still seemed crazy—unbelievable. Even though she had thought of little else these past few weeks.

It was difficult not to when faced with a daily cocktail

of drugs and injections, but she had never allowed herself to get past this stage—past the actual implantation of the embryo. She couldn't put it off much longer. At some point she was going to have to confront the reality of what she was doing. Whether she was pregnant or not pregnant there were going to be life-changing consequences. And at the moment all of them seemed equally scary.

Rafael was waiting for Lottie on the steps of the clinic and kissed her formally on the cheek. They walked in through the sliding glass doors together.

He looked tall and handsome, wearing a dark grey suit and white shirt, open at the collar, a grey silk tie pulled loose. Lottie was struck afresh by the sheer force of his beauty, his charismatic presence and style. Even in the few days since she had seen him his injuries had healed more rapidly—the bruises faded to a pale yellow beneath his olive skin, the whiplash scar a pale pink line.

They exchanged a silent glance as they stood in the reception area, Rafael's armour plating of control firmly in place, Lottie's mouth too dry to say anything even if she had wanted to.

Dr Oveisi arrived, and as the three of them got into a lift to go up to the third floor he wasted no time in informing them that the assisted hatching of the frozen embryo had been successfully completed and everything was good to go. The expression of relief on Rafael's face was reflected in the mirrored walls around them.

And so it was that, less than half an hour later, the whole procedure had been completed.

Lottie hadn't wanted Rafael to be there—had tried to persuade him that he might prefer to stay in the waiting room, suddenly feeling ridiculously shy in front of him. But, fastening the green scrubs behind his back, he had merely given her a contemptuous look that had needed no words to clarify it. And she had to admit his presence had helped; like a towering wall of determination, it had felt as if his will alone was enough to make this work.

And when he had reached for her hand she had found herself gripping it as if her life depended on it. Or at least their baby's life.

Now he stood behind her as they stared at a computer screen and the doctor ran the scanner over Lottie's stomach, pointing out the tiny bubble of air showing where the embryo had been placed. Lottie stared at it, sending out all the positive vibes she could, willing it to do what it had to do.

'Now...' Dr Oveisi turned to look at the prospective parents. 'There are a few rules you will need to abide by for the next couple of weeks.'

From her prone position, Lottie nodded.

Rafael waited, sharp and alert.

'I am a firm believer that stress is the body's worst enemy when it comes to successful embryo implantation, and as such it should be avoided at all costs. Research is only just beginning to discover how important the right mental state of the recipient is. By that I don't mean that the Contessa should take to her bed and do nothing—far from it.' He looked directly at Lottie. 'I want you to use the next couple of weeks to do the things that give you pleasure—activities that will take your mind off the outcome of the procedure. So moderate exercise, mental stimulation and full marital relations are all advisable.'

Marital relations? The very air in the room seemed to gasp at the thought of it. That was the one thing Lottie could guarantee wasn't going to happen.

The sad absurdity of the situation forcefully struck her once again.

Finally Rafael and Dr Oveisi left the room, leaving Lottie to stay in bed for the requisite fifteen minutes. Gazing into space, she felt a myriad of conflicting and confusing thoughts crowd her mind. Had that really just happened? Was she really lying here with their embryo implanted inside her?

Up and dressed, and feeling a bit more in control, she went down to the reception area. The twin stares of the two receptionists alerted her to where Rafael stood, leaning against the wall, one long leg crossed over the other, talking into his mobile phone.

Seeing Lottie he gestured her towards him.

'Oui, oui, d'accord, deux semaines.' He raised his eyebrows at her before returning to his call, speaking in rapid French.

Lottie had always been confounded by the way he could do that—switch from one language to another with seamless ease. Fluent in English, French and German, as well as his native Italian, it seemed to be as natural to him as breathing.

As she waited for him to finish she suddenly had a vivid flashback. The two of them snuggled up together in the ridiculously narrow bed of the tiny student flat she had been renting when they'd first met, with the diffused afternoon sun filtering through the cheap cotton curtains. Rafael had been teasing her about her schoolgirl French, making her repeat words after him as he trailed his fingers down her naked skin, following them with a line of feather-light kisses. As each word had become more erotic than the last he'd finally claimed her pouting lips with his own, and the lesson had ended with something that was certainly never taught in school.

'Bene—everything is sorted.' Slipping the phone into his trouser pocket he turned, frowning slightly as he no-

ticed the flush on Lottie's cheeks. 'I've arranged a little trip away for us.'

Lottie readjusted her face. 'What do you mean?'

'We are going to Villa Varenna. I thought you might like that.'

'Well, yes…maybe.'

Now it was Lottie's turn to frown. The Revaldis had property all over the place, but this was her favourite— a beautiful villa, perched on the side of a stunning Italian lake.

'When were you thinking of going?' It seemed a strange time to be considering a holiday, when their lives were on hold until they knew if she was pregnant.

'Now.' Rafael's beautiful dark eyes regarded her calmly.

'Now?' Lottie repeated incredulously. 'How could we possibly go now?'

'Easy. I've already got the helicopter here. We can be there in a couple of hours.'

'But we can't. I mean—not now. I don't have any things…clothes, toiletries.'

'You're not seriously telling me you can't go because you don't have a toothbrush?'

Lottie gave him her best imperious stare. Just because he had come over all Mr Spontaneous, it didn't give him the right to mock her.

'I am just trying to be practical. What about the car— the one I drove here in?'

'All sorted.' He dismissed her concerns with a wave of his hand. 'There is really nothing to get worked up about.'

'I am not worked up.' She modulated her voice accordingly. 'How long would we go for?'

'Until we know for sure that you are pregnant.'

'Two weeks!' The voice soared again. 'Surely you can't just drop everything and go away for two weeks?'

'There are such things as computers, Lottie, and phones and modern technology. I'm not suggesting we paddle up the Amazon and live in a mud hut. I can work quite well from the villa. Neither am I suggesting that we drop everything, come to that. Let me put your mind at rest on that score.'

Well. That was her firmly put in her place.

'There is one thing, though. The villa is unstaffed, with this being a spur-of-the-moment decision. There is no one around. I could arrange it, of course, but I've decided not to bother. I thought we might enjoy having the place all to ourselves.'

CHAPTER FOUR

SITTING ON THE terrace of Villa Varenna was like having been transported to a different world. Only a few hours ago she had been lying on a hospital bed, staring at the central heating ducts. Now dusk was turning into night over Lake Varenna and the colourful lights of the properties scattered along the shoreline were glittering like a necklace of jewels. As the sky turned a milky blue against the jagged black shapes of the mountains the water was transformed to a luminous purple.

Lottie had never been able to get used to this—the sheer wealth and privilege of the Revaldi family. It was so far removed from her own upbringing she had never felt comfortable with it; growing up in a suburban semi had hardly prepared her for *this*. Her life had been all Neighbourhood Watch and twitching curtains—her own mother having given them plenty to twitch about when she had arrived back from yet another *little holiday* with a suntanned gentleman and a giftwrapped memento of some exotic place she had no doubt viewed from the deck of a cruise ship.

It was different for Rafael, of course; he had been born into this lifestyle—it was a part of him, who he was. And along with the wealth and privilege came an enormous amount of commitment and hard work. Lottie had seen for herself the weight of responsibility that came with the title of Conte di Monterrato—a title that had passed to Rafael on the death of his father.

Lottie had never met her father-in-law, Georgio Revaldi. He had died suddenly when she and Rafael were still living in Oxford, effectively ending their fairytale life there and then. Because that was what it had been, Lottie now realised. A Rafe and Lottie fairytale—a glorious, passionate, heady love affair that had been far too perfect to make it in the real world. It had been inevitable that the story would come to an end, that the book would eventually slam shut.

They had met one drizzly afternoon in Oxford when Rafael had appeared through the steam of the espresso machine in the coffee bar where Lottie had worked. Two hours, several cups of coffee and an impatient queue of customers had seen them briefly sketch in their lives to each other. Rafael had been finishing his business doctorate at the university; Lottie had ben in her third year at art school. It had seemed the most natural thing in the world that he would wait for her to finish her shift, that they would then run together through the full-on rain to Rafael's favourite English pub and arrive, laughing and dripping over the towelling bar mats, already totally and recklessly in love.

Because it *had* been reckless—especially Lottie getting pregnant so quickly. Even though they had been thrilled—speechless with joy, in fact—it had meant a hastily arranged wedding in an Oxford register office, and in retrospect Lottie could see that was hardly what Rafael's father would have wanted for his only son and heir. That in all probability she was not what he would have wanted for his only son and heir.

But she'd never had the chance to find out because

Georgio had died shortly after their wedding and that was when everything had changed. Rafael had hastened back to Monterrato, taking with him his pregnant bride, throwing Lottie into the totally unfamiliar role of wife of the Conte. And with the principality seeming to take up all of Rafael's time cracks had started to appear in their relationship even before the tragedy of Seraphina's death.

Lottie had been lonely, resentful of this wretched place Monterrato which had stolen the husband she had fallen in love with in England and replaced him with a workaholic businessman.

And nothing had changed now. The principality of Monterrato still came first. The only reason she was here was to protect its future, provide an heir. But even with that realisation gnawing away at her she couldn't hold back her excitement as she spread her hands across her stomach. That heir might…just might…be starting life inside her now.

Hearing a sound behind her, she turned to see Rafael coming towards her, carrying a blanket over his arm.

'I thought you might need this.' Shaking it out, he went to spread it over her knees, but Lottie edged further along the bench to stop him.

'I'm not an invalid, you know.'

'I know. I just thought you might be cold.'

'Well, I'm not.'

'Okay. Just bad-tempered then.' Whipping back the blanket, he threw it over one shoulder and looked down at her. 'What would you like to do tonight?'

Lottie darted a look at him, his shadowed figure tall and imposing as he stood there, matador-like, waiting for her answer. Surely he wasn't expecting them to do anything *else* today, was he? Wasn't an embryo transplantation followed by a helicopter ride to this place enough for one day?

'Do?'

'I mean about food.' His eyes glowed in the dark. 'Do you want to go out for a meal?'

'No, thank you. I'm actually quite tired. Not invalid tired—just…well, tired.'

'Yes, of course. I should have thought. In that case I will cook something for us.'

'You really *are* determined to make me an invalid, aren't you?'

The barb hit its target and Rafael pursed his lips against a spreading smile. 'That was uncalled for, young lady.' He regarded Lottie in the dying light. 'And, besides, I hardly think you are in a position to make accusations. Unless you have recently acquired some skills that were hitherto sadly lacking?'

'I may have done.' Lottie raised her chin in challenge. She hadn't, in fact—she was still as useless as ever in the kitchen. But he didn't have to know that.

'Well, in that case I will look forward to some gourmet meals during our fortnight here.'

Lottie's heart lurched inside her. However was she going to survive two weeks here, alone with Rafael? Looking at him standing there, feeling the watchful gleam of his dark eyes, food was the least of her worries.

'Shall we go in now?'

'In a minute. I just want to sit here a little longer.'

Indicating that she should budge up, Rafael sat down beside her.

Actually she had meant sit here *alone*. Suddenly the bench seemed ridiculously small for two people—especially when one of them was six feet four, with the musculature of someone who was no stranger to the gym.

'It *is* beautiful, isn't it?'

Edging a little further away from him, Lottie pointedly commented on the view, watching the way the colours of the water had changed to an inky blue. The sky was still several shades lighter, the first stars starting to pierce its skin. The fact that she was sharing it with someone who was making every nerve-ending in her body stand to attention was neither here nor there.

'*Si, molto bella.*'

Lottie held her breath as his arm slid along the back of the bench behind her.

'I thought perhaps you could do some painting while you are here.'

'Maybe.' Her breath came out with a huff. The arm behind her suddenly felt controlling, domineering, even if the idea of painting again did excite her. It had been so long since she had done any of her own work. And this would be the perfect place to paint.

'You mustn't give up, you know.' Misinterpreting her coolness Rafael held the back of the bench and swivelled round to face her, his knee touching her thigh. 'You have a considerable talent. It would be such a waste not to use it.'

'I'll bear that in mind.' Her acerbic reply was in no small part a response to the intimacy of his closeness in the dark, to the way she could feel the heat coming off his body, hear his breath as it met the cold air.

'Come on.' Standing upright, he gestured to her to do the same. 'We need to go inside and get you some food. Perhaps that will improve your temper.'

The kitchen was sleek and modern, all polished concrete and brushed steel. At first sight it appeared devoid of anything edible, but opening the fridge revealed that it was fully stocked with eggs, milk, cold meats and cheese, and the larder contained an impressive array of packets and tins, all neatly lined up for their inspection.

'I arranged to have a few supplies brought in.' Rafael's voice came from inside the fridge. 'What do you fancy?'

'I don't know.' Momentarily sidetracked by his rear view, Lottie looked away. 'Omelettes?'

'Good idea.' Coming out with the eggs, he proceeded to open every drawer and cupboard in the room before coming up with a bowl, a frying pan and a whisk.

Lottie perched herself on a stool at the island unit as Rafael moved around the kitchen gathering his ingredients. She was secretly enjoying this—not just the novelty of having him cook for her but being able to watch him do it, to let her eyes follow him around when he was too distracted to return her stare, match it with his own.

'Anything I can do to help?'

He was chopping peppers now, the knife coming down hard and fast on the wooden board. This was the point when Lottie had to look away—she'd never liked the sight of blood.

'You can open the wine if you like.'

'I think I might stick to water.'

Suddenly the knife paused, the blade glinting in midair. As Rafael pushed the hair back from his marked forehead Lottie could see the enormity of the day's events reflected in his eyes.

She gulped back a sudden lump in her throat. 'But I will pour a glass for you.'

One smoke alarm, a medley of half-cooked vegetables and a burnt omelette later, their meal was finally finished.

Laying down her knife and fork, Lottie looked across at the man on the stool beside her, trying to figure out what was going on in his head. Dark, complicated, charming, ruthless, passionate, controlling—he was all of those things and more. He hadn't changed, and no matter how much she tried to ignore it, Lottie knew that neither had her desire for him. He looked so handsome when he was relaxed like this, one leg bent, a scruffy leather boot resting on the bar of the stool, his faded jeans pulled taut against his powerful thigh. He was like a deadly potion, begging to be drunk.

'Well, thank you. That was….interesting.' Eyebrows raised innocently, she blinked at him.

'It was terrible, wasn't it?' Tearing at a hunk of dry bread, Rafael, obviously still hungry, put a piece in his mouth and chewed, his strong jawline moving rhythmically. 'But before you mock don't forget it's your turn tomorrow. Your chance to show me these new-found skills.'

'I never said they were *culinary* skills.' Letting her guard slip for a moment, Lottie batted back what was meant to be a light-hearted quip, but Rafael instantly stiffened, twisting round on the stool to face her.

'So what other skills might we be talking about?' His voice was suddenly hard, probing, the whole mood having changed in an instant.

'None—nothing.' Lottie frowned at him. 'I was just messing about.'

'*Have* you been messing about, Lottie?' Rafael's eyes bored into her, scanning her face for answers. 'That's what I want to know.'

'Rafe, stop this. That's not what I meant and you know it.'

'But there have been other men?'

Suddenly angry, Lottie reared up. 'I think you will find that is none of your damned business.' She could feel the heat sweeping across her cheeks, temper mixed with indignation and defiance shooting violet sparks into her icy blue eyes as she held her body taut. 'And besides, why do you even need to ask? Haven't your nasty little private investigators already given you all the information you need? In fact, why don't you tell *me* what I've been up to? You probably know more than I do.'

'Now you are being ridiculous.'

'So nothing, eh? Your grubby little spies could uncover nothing?' She glared at him. 'But it's still left you wondering, hasn't it? Whether maybe they missed something—maybe I do have a lover tucked away that you know nothing about?'

'And do you?' His voice was lethally low, his eyes warning her that she was entering very dangerous territory with this taunt.

'No. I don't, as it happens. But what if I did? What right do you have to poke your nose into my love-life when no doubt *you* have had a string of women in your bed?' She paused, her pent-up breath swelling her breasts as she dared him, *willed* him to deny it.

But he just continued to glower at her, his egotism, his gall, the downright sexual arrogance of him fuelling her outrage and jealousy, bringing bile to the surface.

'Any women I might have had are none of *your* damned business.' The weight of his words broke the cruel silence.

Slipping off her stool, Lottie knew she had to get away from him. She was *not* going to fling herself into that bear-pit of torture. Not today, at any rate.

'I'm going to bed.'

Suddenly he was beside her, pulling her towards him, locking his arms around her unyielding body in the steel ring of his embrace.

'Get off me.'

She struggled to free herself from his arms but then stopped when the contact between them threatened to take a different, much more worrying turn. As he loosened his grip slightly, just enough to pull back and look into her face, Rafael's blazing stare told her that he had felt it too.

Dropping his arms, he turned his back, walked away from her. 'I think you need to remember what Dr Oveisi said.' He spoke coldly over his shoulder. 'You really shouldn't get yourself all worked up, you know. It's not good for you...' He paused, hesitating over his choice of words. 'Or for the chances of the pregnancy working.'

Could he be more arrogantly, impossibly infuriating? Lottie didn't know what enraged her the most. His audacity in cross-examining her about her love-life or the patronising way he thought he could control her.

'Don't you dare start telling me how to behave.' She fired off the words at the broad expanse of his back. 'You started this fight—twisting my words, cross-examining me about my love-life. You are the one that needs to think about their behaviour.'

'I suggest you try and get a good night's sleep.' Turning round, Rafael levelled cold dark eyes in her direction. 'I'm sure you will feel better in the morning.'

Wandering out on to the terrace, Rafael followed the pathway down towards the ornate iron gates that opened directly onto the lake. Turning the heavy old key in the lock, he let the gates swing open and descended the steep flight of steps down to the water, his footsteps hollow against the worn stone. A row of striped mooring poles stood to attention in front of him, the furthest one having a sleek speedboat tethered to it, the water gently slapping at its sides.

Seating himself on the boardwalk, Rafael let his legs hang over the water, absently staring down into the rippling blackness.

Today had seen the first stage of his mission accomplished. His only hope of fatherhood had finally been given its chance of life. Whether it worked or not was now down to the tiny blob of cells, five days' worth of shared genes, set free from its frozen prison, free to make its own decision about the future.

He should have been feeling elated—jubilant. This had

been his goal ever since he had been delivered the devastating news that the accident had rendered him sterile. But there was no elation, just anger—with himself and with the situation.

What had he been thinking, getting into an argument with Lottie on the very first evening? Wasn't he supposed to be making this a stress-free fortnight? It had come out of nowhere, that primal jealousy—fury, even—that she might have been with another man. He couldn't think about it, couldn't bear to go there. His investigations had revealed nothing, and she had said there was no one. He had to leave it at that.

But still the thought of her in the arms of another man tortured him as viciously now as it had when she had first left him. The idea that some bastard might have taken her to his bed, touched her, made love to her, poured a river of molten lava through his veins.

It wasn't as if *he* had remained celibate. Lottie was right. There *had* been other women—probably not as many as she imagined, but women who had shared his bed, satisfied his needs. But none of them had meant anything. Since the day Lottie had left him, the day she had told him she had never loved him, it was as if that part of him had died—the part that was capable of really feeling, the part that was capable of love.

But now that Lottie was back in his life he realised that the feelings he had thought were dead—had been *sure* were dead, in fact—were just buried, deep down inside him. Seeing her again, spending time with her, had brought them all back up to the surface, leaving them exposed to the elements like blind earthworms, ready to be pecked at by a circling crow.

Well, that was *not* going to happen. No matter how alluring she might be, how the turn of her head or the tilt of her chin might take him straight back to the lovely young woman he had fallen in love with, how unconsciously sexy, how damned infuriatingly, *grabbably* gorgeous she was… he was *not* going to open his heart to her again. After all, hadn't she spelled out her feelings clearly enough to him? Or lack of them, at any rate. What sort of fool would go back for a second helping of *that*?

Upstairs in the cream and white-painted bedroom, Lottie, wearing the sensible cotton nightie that had been mysteriously laid out for her, slipped into the freshly made bed, propping the pillows up behind her. Her head felt as if it might explode with everything that had happened that day. Pulling the duvet under her chin, she drew her knees up to her chest and hugged them tightly, trying to find some rational logic, something to justify the crazy madness of it all.

Except, of course, there was none. Rational logic would have screamed at her not to do this, to get straight back on a plane to England and flee the deadly cocktail of longing and torment that was Rafael Revaldi. Rational logic would have saved her from the way she felt now, her whole body churning with impotent resentment and powerlessness.

How dared he come over all caveman like that? What right did he have to challenge her about her love-life when she knew for a fact that he had scores of beautiful and eligible women throwing themselves at his finest leather handmade shoes? She had had to accept it, even if it did still hurt like a knife stabbing her in the gut.

It wasn't as if she had actually been seeing anyone—not seriously. There had been dates—nice young men who'd wanted to take things further, with earnest declarations of love, even, but none of them had come close to affecting her. She simply couldn't relate to them. Not after a real man. Not after Rafael. She was quite resigned to the fact that he had been the one and only man for her. She had always known it.

It was what had made leaving him the hardest thing she had ever done in her life.

But she had had to find the strength to walk away. Their future together had died along with Seraphina—despite or maybe because of Rafael's obsession with getting her pregnant again. It had been as if a baby would be the only thing to validate their marriage, that without a child he would have to face up to the reality of the situation. That he should never have married her. That she was a mistake.

Her bed was positioned opposite the window, with views over the lake and the mountains beyond. Lottie had left the shutters open, and now she slipped out of bed and padded over to the window to look out. She could just make out a dark figure locking the iron gates down by the water, then moving purposefully up the terrace pathway towards the villa.

Retreating into the shadows of the room, Lottie watched as Rafael's imposing shape came closer until he stopped abruptly and looked up at her window. Gripping the window frame, Lottie stared back at him. Their eyes locked for a moment. Then with a curt nod of his head he started walking again, until the villa hid him from view.

CHAPTER FIVE

For a second when Lottie opened her eyes the next morning she couldn't remember where she was. Light was streaming into the room, and the picture-perfect view of the mountains and sky was like a painting, hanging on the wall before her.

But mad reality soon flooded back, nudging aside the blissful ignorance of sleep and replacing it with a checklist of worries. The embryo transfer, being here at Villa Varenna, two whole weeks closeted with Rafael, not to mention his boorish behaviour last night... They had almost come to blows within hours of being here, for heaven's sake. That hardly boded well for the rest of their stay.

Slipping out of bed, she went into the bathroom, stopping as she caught sight of herself in the full-length mirror. Her long blonde hair fell about her shoulders in sleep-ruffled chaos and her eyes, still drowsy with sleep, squinted back at her. Stepping back, she surveyed herself from the side, smoothing down the fabric of her nightie over her very flat stomach.

What was going on in there? Could she be pregnant? Was it really possible?

The realisation of how much she wanted this baby was shocking, dizzying. An outsider might have assumed she was doing this for Rafael—her final gift to him, a last attempt to atone for the brutal way she had walked out on him. Why else would she consider condemning herself to a loveless marriage solely for the sake of bearing him a child? But the outsider would be wrong. She wanted this baby—wanted it with every fibre of her being. Not to help Rafael out of his predicament, not out of guilt or selfless-ness, and certainly not because she cared about providing an heir for Monterrato. She wanted this baby for herself. It was her chance of motherhood. To be the mother she had always wanted to be.

Uttering a few silent words of encouragement to her tummy, she stepped into the shower and let the powerful jets of water pummel all thoughts from her head.

'Buongiorno.' Rafael looked up from his laptop as Lot-tie entered the kitchen, registering the cloud of freshly washed curls, the floral scent of shower gel. She was wear-ing a flimsy cotton dressing gown belted so tightly around her waist it was in danger of cutting her in two. 'Your things have arrived. I'd have brought them up, but I thought maybe you needed a lie-in.'

'How considerate.' She winced at her own acerbity. Today was supposed to be a new day, with the bitterness of yesterday put behind her.

'I hope you slept well?' Ignoring her ill temper, he pulled out a stool for her. He was wearing a white shirt, the sleeves rolled up above the elbow to reveal muscular olive-skinned forearms, liberally dusted with dark hair.

'Yes—fine, thank you.'

'Are you hungry?' He gestured to the plate of pastries beside him.

'Umm…'

He slid the plate towards her and watched as she seated

herself next to him, carefully arranging the dressing gown to cover her legs.

'They do look nice.'

'*Cornetti*, fresh from the *panificio*. I took the boat out early this morning.'

Slicing open one of the pastries, she spread it thickly with butter and took a bite.

'So, how are you feeling?' Closing his laptop, Rafael turned to give her his full attention, distracted by the grease-slicked swell of her pink lips as she chewed hungrily.

'If you mean by that do I feel pregnant, then, no—I feel just the same as yesterday.' She concentrated on her eating.

'Actually, I meant has your mood improved?' Every now and then he could glimpse the tip of her tongue, disappearing into the dark moistness of her mouth. 'But I guess you have answered that.'

'My mood is perfectly all right, thank you.' Wiping her fingers on a piece of paper towel, she tipped her chin to look at him.

'Good…good.'

He leant forward, watching her eyes widen as he did so, and removed a flake of pastry stuck to her lower lip, then sucked it off his finger. The intimacy of the gesture shocked him. What did he think he was doing? Lottie looked equally startled, immediately pulling back.

'You don't have to be like this, you know,' she said. Holding the collar of her dressing gown, she pulled it more tightly across her chest.

'Like what?'

'I don't know… Like, well…falsely polite.'

'Meaning…?' He stared at her.

'What I'm saying is, don't feel that you have to pussy-foot around me for the whole two weeks. It wouldn't feel right—and anyway the strain will kill you.'

'Pussyfoot?' He watched the blush spread across her cheeks as she looked down, moving pastry crumbs around on the plate with her finger. The word seemed to have taken on a far more carnal meaning. 'I had no idea that was what I was doing.'

'I just mean that we need to try and be normal.' She turned to look at him again, still fighting to control the colour of her skin. 'We both know the situation; it's not as if we need to pretend to each other. Playing the part of dutiful husband is not going to make me any more pregnant and it would just feel like a sham.'

'Well, thank you for pointing that out.'

As her sharp words hit home Rafael narrowed his eyes at her. It was obvious what she was doing: setting the ground rules, constructing a safety barrier between them to keep his unwanted attentions away. Just the idea that she thought she had to do that curdled his stomach.

'Fine.' His voice was harsh, cutting. 'I agree that we don't want there to be any misunderstandings between us. Like we might enjoy each other's company, or anything like that.'

Now it was Lottie's turn to feel the chill. Why was she being made to feel bad for pointing out the truth? The hostility he had shown her when she had first arrived back at the *palazzo* had demonstrated clearly enough what he thought of her.

'I think it's important that we are honest with each other, that's all. I know what Dr Oveisi said, and everything, but that doesn't mean we should be trying to fool each other.'

'Whatever you say.' Bored with the subject, Rafael stood up, fixing Lottie with a steely stare. 'Have you finished your breakfast?'

Well, *that* awkward conversation was obviously over. 'Yes, thank you. I'll go and get dressed now.'

'Wait.' He watched an immediate flicker of wariness cross her blue eyes. 'I have something to show you first.'

'You do? What's that?'

'Come with me and you will find out.'

There was a beat of hesitation before Lottie slipped down from the stool, a flash of leg emerging from the unflattering dressing gown.

'I hope you will accept one thing I have planned as a result of Dr Oveisi's advice without feeling the need to argue about it.'

Lottie followed him out of the kitchen and up the stairs, her heart thumping more wildly with every step. What exactly had he planned? Despite telling herself not to be stupid, only one piece of Dr Oveisi's advice clanged loudly in her head. *Full marital relations.* They appeared to be heading for a bedroom. She could feel her traitorous body already bounding ahead of her brain. Surely there was no way he could be thinking…? Could he?

Crossing the landing, Rafael flung open a door and gestured to her to go in before him. Cautiously, Lottie entered.

'What do you think?'

Beside her now, he watched her survey the contents of the room. An artist's easel had been set up in the middle, and a large number of stretched canvases of various sizes were propped against the wall. A palette, a pot of brushes, and a dizzying array of tubes of paint were laid out on a table next to the easel.

'I thought this room might be the best—with the light, I mean. It faces north.'

Lottie stared at it.

'Is something wrong?'

'No—no, of course not.'

'What, then?'

Desperately trying to compose her features in order to

banish any sign of disappointment, Lottie paced around the room. 'It's just that it's a bit over the top.' She attempted a small laugh as she gesticulated around her. 'I mean, we are only here for a fortnight—even Van Gogh couldn't paint this many canvases in two weeks!'

'Who said anything about two weeks? We can leave the room like this and you can come whenever you want—stay as long as you like when you are pregnant. It's beautiful here in the springtime.' Catching the look on Lottie's face, he narrowed his eyes. 'All pregnancy-friendly paints and solvents—I've checked.'

If only it was just the paint that was troubling her. Far more worrying was the way he was insidiously starting to control her life, beginning to manipulate her, make decisions about her future without even consulting her.

And more worrying still was the way her body had soared with excitement at the ridiculously misguided idea that he might be taking her to bed.

'We don't know if I am pregnant yet, Rafael.' Cross with herself, and determined to exert some control of her own, she knew the words sounded harsher than she felt. Moving in front of the window, she planted her bare feet firmly on the floor, yanked the belt of her dressing gown tighter. 'And even if I am, I'd like to remind you that nothing has been decided yet. I have no idea why you are assuming I will be living *here*.'

'Well, not necessarily here…'

'I mean here as in Monterrato. I *do* have a life of my own, you know—a flat, friends, a job.'

That last bit wasn't strictly true, of course. In fact it wasn't true at all. One final phone call from Ibrahim had seen to that. He had been predictably furious that she hadn't obeyed his instructions and been back at work within the week, and somewhere in amongst the shouted tirade she gathered she had been fired.

But funnily enough all she had felt was relief. Her twelve months at the Ibrahim Gallery had become increasingly strained as Ibrahim, a well-known and respected art dealer, had pushed the boundaries of their working relationship further and further. 'Meeting clients' had increasingly involved briefing sessions in a wine bar first, followed by dark taxi rides with him leeringly spreading himself across the leather seat towards her, the sour smell of whisky on his breath. She had made it very clear on more than one occasion that she would certainly *not* be going back to his place for any *debriefing*.

In retrospect, telling him exactly where he could stick his installations might not have been the wisest of moves—especially as his parting shot had been that she would never work in the art world again. Which was probably true. He was vindictive enough to see to that. But she would find something else somehow. She knew that much. She had started over before, and refused to be afraid of the prospect now.

The more pressing problem at the moment was the toweringly dark man staring at her from across the room. Staring at her with such intensity, such heart-racing, piercing concentration, that Lottie could feel it drilling through to her core, where it heated her from the inside with its seductive power.

'I'm sure there is nothing that can't be put on hold.'

The spell was broken and Rafael's bluntly dismissive words brought Lottie back to her senses, her heart-rate spiking with indignation. Why did he always assume that her life was unimportant?

'Once we know for sure that you are pregnant obviously the sensible thing will be for you to stay at Monterrato.'

'Well, your definition of "obvious" is *obviously* not the same as mine.' She stumbled over her tongue-tied sentence. 'What I am saying is, *if* I am pregnant there is no reason for me not to return to England at least until the baby is due.'

'No, Lottie.' His voice was calm and even, like water just before it cascaded over a hundred-metre drop. 'That is *not* how this is going to work. *When* we know for sure that you are pregnant you will be staying at Monterrato. For the whole of your pregnancy.'

The air between then hummed with tension.

'I think I need to point out one very important thing.' Pushing back her shoulders, Lottie placed her hands firmly on her hips. 'I have agreed to try for this baby, Rafael, not given you the right to control my life. You might do well to remember that.'

Dio! Rafael was having trouble remembering anything at the moment. She obviously had no idea, but standing in front of the window in that damned dressing gown Lottie was giving him a perfect silhouette of her body. He had tried not to notice, to look away, but the outline of her waist, the curve of her hips, her long, shapely legs, kept drawing him back. And now she had gone and thrust forward her breasts to taunt him still further.

'You need to get some clothes on.'

He saw Lottie frown at him. At the gruffness of his voice. At the abrupt change of conversation. He knew he had to get away—away from the physical ache of sexual hunger that Lottie stirred in him.

Striding towards the door, he turned and gave her one last glance over his shoulder before marching back down the stairs.

He was heading for the study, but changed his mind. First he needed to do something physical—burn off some of the excess energy that was suddenly pumping through him. The next flight of stairs took him down to the basement, to the gymnasium and indoor pool. Flicking on the lights of the gym, he went over to the dumbbells, picked them up. The weight of them was comforting as he started to flex his muscles. A good workout—that was what he needed, to start getting his body back to the peak of fitness.

He stopped, one dumbbell suspended in the air. Fitness be damned. He snorted at his own deception. Who was he kidding? He needed a workout to rid himself of the image of Lottie and the immediate visceral effect that she had on him.

If he was going to have to put up with much of that temptation over the next two weeks he was going to be spending a *lot* of time in the gym.

Pressing down on the meat in the frying pan, Lottie watched as blood oozed out. She liked her steak charred to a cinder; Rafael liked his rare. Even trying to co-ordinate the food they ate seemed like a struggle.

These past few days at Villa Varenna had been awful, excruciating. Like actors in a play, she and Rafael had moved around this beautiful stage, moved around each other, oscillating between angry disagreement and unnatural politeness and restraint, their wariness of the situation, of the fragility of the arrangement, both painfully obvious and carefully concealed.

Three days in and counting. Lottie seriously wondered how they were going to survive two whole weeks. It wasn't just the pregnancy issue—though Lord knew that filled her mind every waking minute, seeped into her dreams at night. Mentally she veered erratically between exhilaration and desperation, depending on which imagined outcome had gripped her in its talons at the time.

The hardest part was simply being around Rafael, sharing the same space as him, realising the way he could still make her feel—the way she knew deep down that she had always felt. The two years of separation, the countless lectures she had given herself, were all washed away on a tide of longing when she was presented with him again in the flesh.

The beautiful, haughty, honed and hard-edged flesh that was Rafael.

Over the hiss of the pan she could hear him moving about in the next room, then music coming through the sound system above her head. Opera. *La Traviata*—sad and Italian. What was he trying to do to her?

'Ready yet?' Rafael strode restlessly into the room, wearing black jeans and a loose black shirt with the sleeves rolled up in his casual, infuriatingly handsome way.

'Nearly.' Lottie flipped over her steak. 'Can't we have something a bit more cheerful?' She indicted the music with a pained tilt of the head.

He disappeared again and there was a brief silence before Johnny Cash and his burning ring of fire started up.

'I thought this would go with your steak.' He was behind her now, looking over her shoulder. 'Or what's left of it. Is this one mine?' He indicated the plate beside the hob.

'Yes.' She shifted her position to block his view. 'It's resting.'

'Right.' Reaching over her to pick up the plate, he viewed it suspiciously.

The ensuing silence was enough to make Lottie spin round with the fish slice in her hand. 'Is there a problem?'

'*No, di certo*—absolutely not. Shall I take the salad through?'

They had taken to eating at the small table by the bay window of the sitting room. The views of the lake were a useful distraction from the inadequacies of the food, not to mention the inadequacies of their conversation. None of the big issues had been broached by either of them since their disagreement in the studio yesterday, and the practicalities of what would happen if Lottie was actually pregnant were being avoided like a minefield in a war zone.

For her part, Lottie had decided there was no point in getting into another argument with Rafael about something that might never happen. She had no intention of making this enforced captivity any more excruciating than it already was.

'How has the painting gone today?' Cutting into his steak, Rafael raised his fork to his mouth and his all-seeing gaze to her face.

'Good.' Lottie felt the familiar clench in her stomach at the sight of him. She struggled with an awkward mouthful of salad. 'I'm only doing small studies at the moment; I'm hoping I can scale them up to a bigger painting.' She paused as she caught the look in his eyes. 'That's if I'm here long enough, I mean.'

Rafael's jaw clenched but he said nothing.

'Trying to catch the light on the water is incredibly difficult.' She hurried on to avoid that particular quagmire. 'Just when I think I am getting somewhere I look up again and it's all changed.'

'A bit like life, really.' Rafael coldly turned his attention back to his meal.

Lottie looked down at hers.

'Had you been doing much painting since...since we last saw each other?'

Lottie noted his tactful turn of phrase, and his voice was even, but it was belied by the tautness of his body, as if he was holding back the desire to jump on his chair and scream *Since you walked out on me.*

'Um, no, not really. I've not had much time, what with

a full-time job and everything.' She chased a cherry to-mato round her plate. 'I've kept up my drawing, though. In fact I've been doing a lot of sketches—you know, just for friends... portraits, treasured pets, that sort of thing.'

'I'm glad you have been using your talent. So, this job of yours...'

Laying his knife and fork down, Rafael steepled his fingers over his plate and fixed her with his most piercing gaze. Lottie braced herself for an interrogation, immediately on the defensive.

'Tell me how it is, working for a guy like Ibrahim?'

'It's okay.' She shrugged her shoulders. 'The job is well paid.' *Was well paid*, she thought silently.

'And what exactly does he expect for his money?'

'What are you suggesting, Rafael?' Her eyes flashed dangerously.

'I'm not suggesting anything.'

'Good, because if you were it would be deeply insult-ing.'

'I'm simply trying to understand why you would flatly refuse a settlement from me in favour of working for a jerk like him.' His lack of understanding was all too evi-dent in the jut of his jaw. 'If you needed money you only had to ask.'

Lottie thought back to the obscene amount of money she had been offered by his solicitors a few months after she had left him. She'd rejected it without a second thought. It had felt as if he was buying her off: goodbye and good riddance.

'And *I* can't understand why *you* can't see that I want to be independent.'

'Of course. How foolish of me to keep forgetting that.' His voice was laced with sarcasm. 'So, tell me—how does this independence feel, being at the beck and call of that slimy bastard?'

'Better than being a kept woman.' Lottie glared back at him. 'And besides, I am not at his beck and call. I am perfectly capable of handling someone like Ibrahim. I can take care of myself.'

Rafael let his gaze rake over the feisty young woman before him and realised that she was probably right—she *could* take care of herself. She was no longer the innocent twenty-one-year-old he had fallen in love with but someone who, despite her delicate appearance, had the maturity to go with her fiery spirit, to cope with whatever life threw at her. Not that his protective instinct would ever go completely. He knew that despite everything he would still leap in front of a flying bullet for her without a second thought.

'I'm not worried.'

'Good.' Lottie chewed at her lip, very much hoping that was the end of that particular conversation.

'Especially as I know you no longer work for him.' The dark brows were raised infuriatingly.

'You *know*?' Lottie felt her blood pressure soar. 'How do you know?'

Rafael merely shrugged his shoulders in reply.

'Why do I even ask?' Lottie's voice soared to match the blood in her veins. 'I should have worked out by now that you have absolutely no scruples when it comes to prying into my life.'

'In actual fact Ibrahim contacted me.' Rafael's reply was maddeningly calm. 'He was inviting me to an exclusive preview—some conceptual artist that he seemed very excited about. Apparently he has enormous investment potential.'

Lottie glowered at him. 'And why would he contact you?'

'Because I am on his client list, of course. I'm surprised

you don't know that. But, then again, I guess it doesn't matter any more.'

'And presumably the only reason you were on his client list was because you were spying on me?'

Rafael gave a *well, you know...* sort of shrug. 'Anyway, I took the opportunity to mention your name and that's when I found out you were no longer in his employ.'

'And did he tell you why?'

'Funnily enough, he didn't seem to want to discuss you.'

'Then let me enlighten you. Ibrahim fired me because of *this.*' Using both hands, Lottie gestured around her, ending with two index fingers pointing at herself. 'He refused to give me any more time off. Sacked me on the spot.'

'Ah.'

'Yes—so basically I have no job to go back to. But *please* don't think that you have to feel guilty about it.'

'I don't.'

Everything about his easy reply told Lottie that her attempt at sarcasm was totally wasted.

'I was actually thinking that it is one minor complication out of the way.'

Typical! Rafael had managed to turn what was a real worry for her—she had bills to pay, after all, and the rent on her flat for starters—into something to his advantage.

But the more Lottie thought about it the more thankful she actually was that she no longer worked for Ibrahim. She knew she would be able to get another job. If leaving Rafael had done one thing it had taught her independence, made her stand on her own two feet.

Arriving back in England with nothing but a suitcase and an alarmingly small amount of cash, she had made the decision to move to London. She needed a fresh start, away from all the memories that would inevitably haunt her in Oxford. She didn't want Rafael to know where she was either—to track her down, demanding answers. Not that she'd needed to worry about that. Apart from that one email from his solicitors she had heard nothing from him at all. There had just been a big, fat hollow where that part of her life had been. The happiest and the saddest part.

Being alone in London had been horrendous to start with. It had seemed such a lonely place that first winter as she'd desperately tried to find a job and somewhere to live, eventually renting a depressing bedsit, feeding coins into a meter for the hissing gas fire, sleeping with her head under her pillow to try and block out the yelping screams and scary silences of her neighbours. She had thought that winter would never end.

But it had, and it had been followed by a particularly beautiful spring. Which had been even worse. Watching lovers in the park, lying on the grass kissing, parents proudly pushing buggies towards the swings, excited toddlers leading the way... It had felt as if the whole world was happy and in love, deliberately taunting her with its joyfulness.

But time had passed and she had made some friends and found a new job, which had meant she'd been able to afford a better apartment, and suddenly things had started looking up. Slowly, slowly, she'd realised that she was no longer waking to the sick feeling of dread any more. The job at the Ibrahim Gallery had provided her with a good salary, even if the boss had made her skin crawl, and suddenly she'd realised that she had moved on, grown up, was in control of her own life again.

Until she had received Rafael's email. Until her old life had reappeared and thrown up the extraordinary situation that they were in now.

She watched Rafael as he leant away from the table, rocking his chair on to its back legs, stretching his arms behind his head. He turned to look out of the window and she could see his reflection in the glass. Dark, shuttered, deep in thought, but as intensely attractive as ever. He wore his beauty casually, as if he didn't notice it even if everyone all around him did. He had no vanity, no interest in showing himself off to the world—just a confidence, an inner belief, an unconscious power that meant he had the ability to achieve whatever he wanted to achieve.

Until the accident.

Lottie was struck again by the enormity of how that must have affected him. She gazed at his chiselled profile, at the whiplash scar which, even though it could never disfigure his beautiful face, was a permanent reminder of what he had suffered.

Since that first day in the office at the *palazzo* he had never talked about the accident. Just as he never talked about anything that mattered. As Johnny Cash's last gravelly note faded to silence she decided to try to get him to open up.

'Tell me about the accident.'

She spoke softly and he swung round to look at her, his guarded expression melting her heart once again.

'What did it feel like, Rafe?'

'It is not an experience I would recommend.' He scraped his chair back sharply, and immediately began to gather up the things on the table. 'Shall I make some coffee?'

He was trying to get away from her, and from any sort of discussion about the accident. But Lottie stopped him.

'In a minute.' Reaching forward, she rested her hand on his forearm, feeling the warmth of his skin, the way his muscles flexed beneath her touch. 'There's no rush.'

As she increased the pressure on his arm she became acutely aware of their skin-on-skin contact, the feel of the dark hairs that were raised beneath her fingertips, before the arm was moved away and folded beneath his other, defensively in front of him.

'What did you feel when you realised that the parachute wasn't going to open?'

Rafael glowered at her. 'What do you *think* I felt?'

'I don't know—that's why I'm asking you.' Stubbornly, she refused to give up.

'Disbelief, horror, panic. Take your pick. There wasn't much time for the existential stuff.'

Still the sarcastic flippancy.

'Did you lose consciousness as soon as you hit the tree?'

'Yes.' He let out an exasperated sigh, seeing that she wasn't going to let this drop. 'I didn't know anything about it until I woke up in a hospital bed, thinking what a bloody fool I was.'

'A fool? I thought you would be feeling pretty darned lucky.'

'Well, that as well. But realising what I had done to myself—the permanent damage, I mean. It could have all been avoided.'

'But you weren't to know—about the parachute, I mean.'

'No. But if I hadn't been jumping from aeroplanes in the first place...' He stopped, as if realising he was giving too much away. 'Anyway, I'm done with all that stuff now.'

Lottie stared at him from beneath the sweep of her lowered lashes. 'You say that now. I bet once you have completely recovered you will be throwing yourself into the path of danger again, every chance you get.'

'Is that what you thought I did?' He looked at her with cold surprise.

Lottie felt herself weaken under his penetrating gaze. 'Kind of. Let's face it—you were always skiing down some mountain or scaling up it or flinging yourself from it. Especially...' she paused '...especially after Seraphina died.'

'You make it sound like some sort of death wish.'

'That's a bit extreme. A diversion tactic, maybe, a form of escapism.'

'Escaping from what?'

'I would have thought that was obvious. From me, from our marriage, from Seraphina's death.'

'*Che assurdità!*' He turned away, muttering something furious in Italian under his breath. 'As usual your amateur psychology has brought you to completely the wrong conclusion. Now, if you will excuse me, I've got some work to do.'

Leaving the plates where they were, he gave her a curt nod before striding from the room, his pride and dignity hurrying to keep up with him.

Was she right? Of course she damned well was. Closing the door to his study, he leant back against it, screwing his eyes shut against the realisation. That was what riled him more than anything—why he hated getting into any so-called conversation with Lottie. The way she wheedled things out of him, picked at subjects that he wanted left alone, attempted to uncover truths that had to stay well and truly buried. Why had he even got into that stuff about giving up action sports?

Even if it was true.

He *had* spent more and more time doing extreme sports over the past few years, turning it from an escapist hobby into an obsession, a way of purging himself. He had told himself he needed something to ease the pressures of running the principality, and there was some truth in that. There had been plenty of times when the massive responsibility had weighed heavily on him and flinging himself off a mountain, as Lottie had so charmingly put it, had given him some release. Pushing himself harder and harder had felt good—addictive, even,—and he'd consoled himself that it was done in the name of a good cause as he had raised huge sums of money for charity.

But there had, of course, been another reason. The one that Lottie had homed in on, jabbing at it like a dentist probing a bad tooth. He knew that the real reason he'd pushed himself harder, further, to take more and more extreme risks, had been because of the adrenalin rush it gave him. And the reason he'd needed that adrenalin was because it had been the only thing that had given him a temporary respite from his feeling of loss. The loss of his baby, his marriage, his wife.

But no more. He'd been given a second chance. A second chance at life and a second chance of producing a life. And he wasn't going to do anything to jeopardise that.

CHAPTER SIX

'COME IN.'

At the soft tap on the door Rafael looked up from his laptop and saw Lottie juggling with a sliding tray, pushing the door open with her hip.

'You mentioned coffee after dinner, so I thought I would bring you some—*us* some.' She indicated the two mugs beside the cafetière.

'Thanks.'

He made no move to clear a space amongst the paperwork strewn around his desk, so Lottie pointedly gave the tray an extra rattle until he got the message.

'There.' She sat herself opposite him and they both watched as Lottie lowered the plunger on the coffee and poured them both a cup. 'You're still working, then?' She held her mug in both hands, inhaling the steam.

'It would certainly appear that way.'

No one could do the arctic chill like Rafael.

'What are you working on?' She picked up a sheet of paper from the desk, feigning absorbed interest, but, sensing his scowl, silently replaced it.

'Nothing you would be remotely interested in. Now, I really don't have time for this, so if you would like to leave…'

'I might be interested if you told me what it was.'

'Why are you here, Lottie?' His sharp words cut through the air between them.

Lottie twisted a curl of hair around her finger. 'I thought maybe we could carry on the conversation we were having earlier. The one you abruptly ended when you walked away.'

'I hardly think you are in any position to criticise me for walking away.' The sharp words came out of nowhere. 'That was something *you* managed to do in a spectacular fashion.'

Ouch! Lottie hadn't seen that one coming. Now she deeply questioned the wisdom of seeking him out. Especially as he was closing his laptop, turning the full force of his dark eyes and even darker mood firmly in her direction.

'That's not what we were talking about.'

'Well, we are now. Since you seem so determined to rake over the past, why don't we examine your part in it?'

'No, Rafe—stop this.'

'How about we start with the night you walked out? Talk me through it, Lottie, the sequence of events, just so I have them clearly in my head.'

'I don't want to do this.'

'Well, too bad—because I do. You wanted to talk, so let's talk. How long had you been planning it, Lottie? Was it a sudden realisation? A spur-of-the-moment thing? Oh, no, it couldn't have been.'

His cruel laugh cut through Lottie like a knife.

'Not when I bear in mind that you had never loved me. You must have been desperate to get away from me— plotting your escape for months.'

He was wrong—so wrong about everything. But Lottie refused to go there, refused to face the coal-black intensity of his piercing eyes and rake over that dreadful night. Even though every single minute of it was seared on her soul for ever.

The hardest decision of her life had been made quickly. The negative result of their third IVF attempt had finally tipped her over the edge, driving the last nail into the coffin of their marriage.

A phone call to the airport had seen her stuffing a small suitcase with clothes and creeping down the steps to a waiting taxi. It had been dark, and even though she'd known Rafael wasn't in the *palazzo* she had winced at the noise of the idling engine, the slam of the doors before they'd finally driven off, Lottie wide-eyed and silent, hunched in the back of the car.

Completely numb with the enormity of her decision, she had been waiting for her flight, gazing at her reflection in the wall of windows overlooking the twinkling lights of the runway, when Rafael's dark shape had appeared behind her like an apparition of foreboding.

His mood had been angry, forceful, as he had demanded to know what the hell she thought she was doing. Would it have been different if he had asked her to stay? Shown some compassion, vulnerability, even? She didn't know. But his boorish attitude had only served to reinforce her decision that they were finished—she had to leave.

She'd had to make him see that she wasn't going to change her mind—that he had to go away, leave her alone with her misery. And there had been only one sure-fire way to do that.

She could still see the look on Rafael's face as she had said the words.

With the Tannoy above their heads announcing the final call for her flight, she had dragged up every ounce of bravado and acting ability she had and blurted out the words.

'I don't love you, Rafael, and I never have.' And they were words that had haunted her ever since.

'I'm still waiting, Lottie.'

'And I am going to bed.'

She went to move, but Rafael leant forward to grasp her wrist.

'Oh, no, you're not. Not until we have had this out. I am waiting for you to explain to me what the hell went wrong with our marriage.'

'Do I really need to explain?' Shaking her wrist free, Lottie hid behind her defiant glare.

'Yes, actually, you do. Because obviously I am lacking the power to be able to work it out for myself.'

'Fine.' If attack was the best form of defence she would face him, head-on. 'You were working all the time, and when you weren't you were off somewhere, doing some crazy activity by yourself, *for* yourself. After we lost Seraphina we never took the time to heal. Instead my life became a miserable round of IVF treatments and invasive procedures in your quest for a precious heir, and when they didn't work you just became more distant and more cold. You never paid me any attention and you never wanted to talk to me. I was lost and lonely and miserable.'

Swallowing down the racking sob that was building up inside her, she covered her face with her hands and felt it shudder through her body.

There was silence.

Through her parting fingers she saw Rafael's face, so twisted with disgust that she had to look away.

She sniff-sobbed loudly. 'Well, you *did* ask.'

'Indeed I did.' His voice was laced with ice. 'And you have certainly delivered. Have you finished now? Or is there more you would like to get off your chest?'

'Yes. Actually, there is.' His coldness and sarcasm only

served to push the floodgates open further. She wanted to hurt him now, the way he was hurting her. 'Our sex-life.'

Rafael's eyes narrowed dangerously. 'Go on.'

'Well…' Lottie gulped down another sniff. 'How can you pretend you thought everything was fine with our marriage when you hadn't even been near me for months?' She paused, aware that she was ripping open her chest to expose her heart, but unable to stop now. 'When you re-alised the IVF wasn't going to work, when you realised I would never give you your precious heir, we didn't even share the same bed any more. You never wanted to make love to me—in fact you never wanted to touch me at all. How do you think that made me feel?'

Rafael looked as if he had been punched in the stom-ach, but Lottie felt no sense of triumph. The intense pas-sion they had shared at the start of their relationship had been so completely overwhelming that Lottie could never have imagined Rafael turning away from her the way he had after Seraphina died. It had tortured her then and it still tortured her now. Especially as she knew, staring at him across the desk now, that those feelings for him were as strong as ever. That her body yearned for him to make love to her again.

Swearing under his breath in Italian, Rafael raked a hand through his hair, what little patience he'd had obvi-ously exhausted. 'You are unbelievable—you know that, Lottie? You have the audacity to come out with this non-sense, pretend that somehow I am at fault for the failure of our marriage, when we both know full well the real reason.'

They stared at one another. Lottie both waiting and dreading to hear what he was going to say next.

'The real reason is because you just didn't care enough. In fact, I don't think you ever cared at all.'

* * *

Lottie shut the door of the villa and walked out on to the terrace. It was a beautiful night, still, star-lit and crisp, but she didn't feel the chill against her skin. Her body was still burning from the heat of their clash, hurt and anguish pumping violently through her veins as she went over and over the things they had said. The ocean of misunderstanding and mistakes and mixed-up longing that lay between them.

Staring out unseeing at the lake, she could feel the anxiety churning around inside her. The consequences of what they had done, the way this could change their lives for ever, were still being ignored by both of them. They had done nothing to sort out their problems, try and find a way through the shared agony of their past, put it right for the future. Instead they avoided the subject or, worse, let it explode between them, just as it had back then, showering them with bitterness and confusion.

What sort of basis was that for bringing a child into the world?

'There you are.'

Rafael was jangling his car keys in his hand when Lottie finally came downstairs. He wore casual jeans and a white tee shirt with a beautifully cut grey linen jacket over the top, a grey cashmere scarf draped around his neck. That unmistakable Italian style he epitomised so well.

'I hope I haven't kept you waiting.'

She'd expected a growled reply but instead was startled to see that he was staring at her, his eyes moving over her in a most disconcerting way.

'What?' She shifted uncomfortably.

Still he didn't say anything, his mouth a tight line, his jaw firmly closed.

Lottie looked down at herself. Why was he staring at her like that?

When Rafael had announced at breakfast that he was taking them out for a meal that evening Lottie's heart had sunk. Was this going to be another torturous evening together, only worse because there would be no escape?

But, conceding that he was trying to make an effort, she'd decided she had to do the same. Maybe between them they could try and improve the brittle atmosphere that had pervaded the villa over the last few days. And, besides, it might be nice to get dressed up for once—swap her paint-splattered jeans for one of the dresses swinging in her wardrobe.

She had been shocked, that first day in the villa, to find along with her own small suitcase, sent over from the *palazzo*, another much larger case, containing several cocktail dresses: vestiges of her previous life with Rafael. The life she had been thrown into so suddenly on the death of Rafael's father and the role she had never been given time to adjust to: the role of Contessa di Monterrato.

Somehow she had assumed Rafael would have got rid of all these clothes—given them away or tossed them into a pile and set light to them. She wouldn't have blamed him. Pulling them out of the rustling tissue paper one by one, she had held them up against herself, remembering the woman she had been when she had worn those dresses, standing beside Rafael at tedious functions, watching the way he could work the room, knowing that every event, no matter what it was called, was simply another public relations exercise—a business meeting in all but name.

They weren't happy memories, and Lottie had quickly selected one garment before pushing the rest, along with the memories, to the back of the closet again.

The dress she had chosen was simple and elegant, made

of a deep blue silk that had an iridescent quality that caught the light as she turned. And, despite its past, it made her feel good. At least it had done until she had been subjected to the full force of Rafael's raking gaze.

Now might have been a time for Rafael to say something complimentary—tell her how nice she looked. Even an appreciative nod would have done.

'You'll be cold.'

So much for that. His deepening frown and the tight pull of his lips suggested nothing but irritation.

'Don't you have a stole or something?'

A *stole*? What century was he living in? They were travelling to a restaurant in his luxury sports car, not a horse and carriage.

'I'm fine.'

She inhaled sharply, suddenly cross with herself. Why had she spent hours trying to make herself attractive to him? Fiddling about with her hair until she perfected the loose bun at the nape of her neck, carefully applying subtle make-up, slithering this dress over her scrubbed and moisturised body. Why the hell had she bothered?

'Put this on, anyway' Stepping towards her, he took off his scarf and, carefully looping it over her hairstyle, arranged it, still warm from his body, around her shoulders.

'Thanks.' Lottie had to move back from him before she could breathe.

Something told her this evening was going to be awful.

But she was wrong. The local restaurant was small and informal, and after the usual amount of fussing and flapping from the staff that always accompanied Rafael wherever he went they were soon seated in a quiet corner, with a single candle flickering on the table between them.

The food was delicious—a selection of freshwater fish served with aromatic sauces and big bowls of fresh pasta.

They both ate hungrily and the conversation flowed surprisingly easily. Rafael started, as he always did, by asking about her day's painting, then actually answered her questions about his day, telling her about his plans for a new marina that was about to start construction, about the vineyards that had to be monitored closely at this time of year, the local elections that had just taken place.

He looked so composed, so handsome, so like the old Rafael she had fallen quite madly in love with.

Lottie tried to concentrate, to focus on the many and varied problems and opportunities obviously involved in being head of a principality like Monterrato. But mostly she found herself being drawn into the hypnotic spell of his deep voice, the way his Italian accent imbued the most mundane of English words with a mantle of sensuality. She watched the way his beautiful mouth moved as he spoke, the bottom lip just that bit fuller than the top one, both biteably, irresistibly kissable. The bruising on his face had faded to almost nothing now, and the scar on his forehead was hidden by a dark twist of hair but still visible where it sliced down the top of his cheekbone. A shadow of stubble darkened his jawline and upper lip; she remembered the feel of that stubble against her cheek, against other parts of her body too...

Enough! She needed to stop this before her internal organs stalled in homage to his beauty. Or, worse still, betrayed her in some hideously embarrassing way. She couldn't even blame it on the alcohol. Sticking firmly to water, she had had no more than a single sip when Rafael had offered her a taste of the local wine he had ordered. You could hardly get drunk on a sip of wine, now, could you? Other forces were obviously at play here—far more dangerous ones.

'Can I ask you something?' Putting his knife and fork

together, Rafael took the napkin from his lap and touched it to his lips. Suddenly his deep brown eyes were focussed intently on her face.

'Yes, of course.' Lottie laughed nervously under his close scrutiny. 'As long as it's not whether I think I might be pregnant.'

Her flippant remark was met with a derisively raised dark brow.

'Because I really have no idea...' She tailed off, registering that this was not a subject he was prepared to be light-hearted about. 'No more idea than you.'

'I realise that.' He rolled his shoulders back, his gaze never leaving Lottie's face. 'I know we have to wait for two weeks before we can do a pregnancy test. That prior to that there are unlikely to be any discernible manifestations. I know the form, Lottie. I haven't forgotten that we've been here before.'

'No, of course not.'

Discernible manifestations? How did he manage to make what they were doing sound so clinical, so detached? Because for him it was, Lottie reminded herself painfully.

'But my question *is* related to that.'

'Go on.'

'Why, Lottie—just to clarify things for me—did you agree to bear me a child?'

Lottie gulped. This was typical of Rafael. Just when things were going peaceably he would lob in a grenade of a question to ruin things. She looked down, the escaping twists of her hair falling forward as she did so, brushing against her cheeks. Even the fish head on her plate looked as if it was waiting for an answer.

'I don't know, exactly.' She raised her eyes again, immediately caught by the net of his gaze. 'I suppose it was a combination of things.'

Rafael ran his hand down his jaw to his chin, leaving it there as he tilted his head to look at her.

'Basically, I suppose you were right when you said you knew I had always wanted to be a mother. It's most probably the maternal instinct in me that made me say yes—as simple as that.'

'These things are never simple, Lottie.'

'Well, perhaps I need to prove that I can be a good mother. A better mother than I had, at any rate.' She smiled at him, not wanting this to get too heavy.

'Well, from what I've heard that won't be difficult. How *is* the lovely Greta?' He raised his eyebrows at her.

'She's very well.' Lottie gave a small laugh. 'As far as I know she and Captain Birdseye are perfectly happy living the high life in Argentina.'

Rafael had never even met her mother. Their early relationship had been such a whirlwind, with Lottie getting pregnant just weeks after she and Rafael had first met, then their hastily arranged wedding and the move to Monterrato—all happening before Greta had managed to find the time to come over. Subsequent invitations had been politely declined because of the *'considerable distance'* between them. Lottie could only agree with that—and she wasn't just thinking about the thousands of miles across the Atlantic.

'I think maybe she has finally found what she was looking for.'

'Let's hope so. And have *you* found what you were looking for?' His gaze swept over her. 'The baby, I mean?'

'We don't know there is a baby yet.' Lottie lowered her eyes, carefully folding her napkin as she tried to inject some realism into the conversation. 'But you falling out of the sky has certainly opened up the possibility, if nothing else. A faint smile touched his mouth.

'So you should be thanking me, really?'

Lottie felt her shoulders drop a little. Could she detect the teeniest sign of a thaw?

'If you like.' She risked another smile, then felt ridiculously hurt when, instead of returning it, he abruptly looked away. 'I suppose what I am saying is that I said yes to using our last embryo because I want this baby every bit as much as you do. Even if my reasons for wanting it are different.'

'What do you mean by that?'

'I mean that my motive is purely emotional—maternal, if you like. Whereas yours is sensible, practical. I know how important it is to you, to Monterrato, that you produce an heir. But that's not why I said yes. I said yes because I want a baby of my own. Nothing more complicated than that.'

Her little speech done, Lottie sat back, sure that Rafael would be relieved. After all, hadn't she just let him off the hook—given him a get-out so that he knew he didn't have to be grateful to her? But she was to be disappointed. Because instead of relief, his look was one of barely controlled temper.

Rafael heard his own pent-up breath hiss between his teeth as he stared across at Lottie. He had thought that going out for a meal would be a good idea—get away from the villa, eat some decent food for once. But he had been wrong. Sitting opposite her now, in the warm and intimate atmosphere of this candlelit restaurant, it no longer felt like a good idea at all.

The evening had started badly when she had first appeared in that flimsy dress. The way the fabric skimmed over her slender body, subtly highlighting the contours of her breasts and hips, then stopping short of her knees to reveal those long, shapely legs... Just the sight of her had all but winded him. And when he had held the door open for her and seen those skinny strap things crossing over her shoulderblades it had taken all his control, and more, not to thread his itchy fingers through them and tear them apart until the dress fell at her feet.

And right now he was still being taunted by her bare shoulders, the shadowed hollows of her collarbone, the elegant sweep of her neck—by everything that she unconsciously did to him. Fighting it was becoming more and more difficult, and he knew he had to use the only weapon in his armoury. Animosity.

'Just for the record—' he spat the words at her '—you are not the only one with emotions, Lottie. You are not the only one to feel things. Despite your cold, calculating opinion of me, I am flesh and blood beneath. Sensible and practical I may be, but that doesn't mean I don't feel things every bit as deeply as you. Perhaps you would do well to remember that.'

'Yes, of course.' Verbally slapped down again, Lottie felt the sting on her cheek as vividly as if he had struck her. 'I didn't mean to imply anything to the contrary. I was just trying to explain the differences between us.'

'That really isn't necessary,' Rafael growled back at her. 'I would have thought the differences were all too clear.'

'Yes.'

Biting down on her lip, Lottie fought to supress the pain of his angry words. The pain of knowing just how true it was that whilst Rafael still stirred up overwhelming longing and desire in her, she only evoked bitterness and resentment in him. She cast about for a suitably acerbic reply—something she could hurt him with as he had hurt her—but it was too late. Turning away, Rafael had already called for the bill.

CHAPTER SEVEN

RAFAEL WOKE WITH a start. He could hear something—a noise somewhere in the villa. As he slipped out of bed a glance at the clock showed it was two-forty-five a.m. Pulling on his jeans, he walked silently across the landing to Lottie's bedroom. The door was closed and he stood there for a moment, listening. Nothing. She was probably sound asleep; it had been several hours since she had flounced off to bed, refusing his offer of a hot drink, leaving him nursing a whisky and a bad mood.

The evening hadn't ended well—just like every other evening since they had been in this place. Every evening since Lottie had been back in his life, in fact. He knew he was failing miserably when it came to following Dr Oveisi's instructions to make these two weeks as stress-free as possible for Lottie. But there was only one bit of Dr Oveisi's advice that he knew for sure he could fulfil—and all too easily. He was wrestling to control it every second that he spent with Lottie. And each day at Villa Varenna was making it that bit more difficult.

The villa was quiet. Perhaps he had imagined it. After padding down the stairs he stood in the hallway, straining his ears. Yes, there it was again, coming from the basement.

A plan was immediately forming in his head. If he could

get into the gym he could grab one of the dumbbells and clobber whoever it was over the head before they had a chance to get away. He could feel the adrenaline starting to surge through his body. Slowly he crept down. The noise was coming from the pool—he could hear the splashing quite clearly now.

Burglars didn't take a dip before they robbed a house.

Standing in the shadows behind the glass wall, he could make out the shape of Lottie's body moving leisurely through the water, swimming to one end, then pushing off and starting back again. The only illumination came from the submerged pool lights and she looked dark against the bright turquoise of the water, arms and legs elongated by the shadows.

He should go. As he turned away the metal button of his fly tapped against the glass and he froze, casting his eyes down as if to make himself invisible.

'Who's there?'

He could hear the squeak of alarm in her voice. What the hell was he doing, lurking in the gloom?

'It's me.' Clearing his throat, brusquely he moved along to the glass door, pushing it open authoritatively. 'I heard a noise. Came down to see what it was.'

'Oh.' She stared at him for a minute before swimming over to the edge of the pool and hanging on with fingertips that were level with his bare feet. 'You scared me.'

'Sorry.'

He looked down at her head and shoulders, streaming with water, her hair slicked back darkly over her forehead and then fanning out around her like seaweed. Closer inspection revealed that beneath the blue of the water she was naked. *Dio.*

He looked away with a jolt. 'What on earth are you doing here at this time of night anyway? You realise that it's nearly three a.m.?' Gruffness covered the growl of desire.

'I couldn't sleep.' She pushed off from the edge of the pool, took a couple of strokes, then stopped to look at him again, treading water. 'I decided to take a midnight swim. A three a.m. swim,' she corrected herself.

The idea had come to Lottie after several hours of fitful tossing and turning. Their evening out had ended on such a sour note, with a silent drive back to the villa and Rafael refusing even to look at her as he headed for the kitchen to fix himself a drink. Lying in bed, staring at the moonlit shadows on the ceiling, she had tried to work out just where it had gone wrong—why it always went wrong.

She had heard Rafael come upstairs, the soft click of his bedroom door. Wide awake, she'd thought back over their time together in the villa: the fraught atmosphere, the tension that had been building and building between them.

She knew that it was more than just the hurt of the past that had caused it, though that would never leave them. It was the raw, fresh assault of the present too. The insidious, sensual, sexual connection that their close confinement had revealed. *That* was what they were both fighting. *That* was what made their time together so unbearable.

Her night-time dip had been a good idea and had made Lottie feel strangely calm. Maybe it was the lack of sleep, but somehow the warm water caressing her naked body had not only washed away her stress but also heightened her sensuality, producing an almost carefree drunkenness. She was in a beautiful place, with a beautiful man, and there was a chance—maybe a good chance—that she was pregnant with his baby.

And now he was here, standing at the edge of the pool, staring at her, the muscular planes of his naked torso shadowed in the dim light. The sight of him stirred an impulsive recklessness in her.

'I'll leave you to it, then.' With one last piercing look Rafael was turning to go.

'Why don't you join me?' Her words had escaped before she knew it, echoing around them and halting Rafael's movement.

He glanced back at her as she bobbed up and down in the water. 'Why would I want to do that?'

'For fun, Rafe. We are supposed to be having fun, remember? It's doctor's orders.' Swimming a few strokes closer, she stopped again and looked at him earnestly, her eyes wide and daring.

Fun. Rafael realised that that was something Lottie had been full of—certainly when he had first met her. It had been one of the many things that had made him love her. She had been so different from anyone he had ever known before—different from the women he was forced to socialise with in Monterrato. Those women were like strategic pawns, carefully chosen because they were the daughters of heads of state or influential businessmen. Part of the reason he had insisted on going to England to do his business doctorate had been to get away from the whole hideous mating ritual.

But he had never expected to find Lottie—never expected to fall so blindly in love and for Lottie to get pregnant so quickly. That had led to the hurried wedding and what now felt like the happiest period of his life. His father had been livid, of course. Rafael still had that furious letter somewhere—their last exchange before Georgio had died of a massive heart attack. Which had to be a coincidence. He was *not* responsible for his father's death. He just wished Georgio had had the chance to meet Lottie. She would have softened his angry heart.

He could see Lottie, waiting, looking up at him, her arms and legs moving silently, tentacle-like, beneath the brightly lit water. She was goading him to join her, probably thinking there was no way in the world that he would. Because he wasn't fun, was he? And, worse than that, he had drained the fun out of Lottie, or at least had a damn good go at it. He could see that now.

Like some vampire of doom he had weakened her carefree spirit, her zest for life, first by throwing her, totally unprepared, into the role of Contessa di Monterrato and then with the death of their baby and his subsequent determination to get her pregnant again. It was a wonder she had any fun left in her at all.

Well, he would show her.

Walking round to the shadows at the far end of the pool, he stripped off his jeans, positioned himself on the edge and with one smooth dive plunged under the water, resurfacing several seconds later right in front of Lottie. And the look on her face was priceless.

Suddenly she was all arms and legs, swimming away from him, but still close enough that he could see her bare buttocks just under the surface of the water.

'Catch me if you can!' The words were sprayed over her shoulder.

She had to be joking. Watching her splash chaotically away, he counted to three before powering after her, beside her again in a couple of crawl strokes. He grabbed hold of her leg as it kicked to escape from him.

Her head went under the water then reappeared and she came up spluttering. 'That's cheating.'

'Don't issue a challenge you can't win, Lottie.' He was tall enough to stand in this part of the pool, but Lottie was still treading water to keep herself afloat, her arms paddling on either side of her. Reaching forward, Rafael placed his strong hands under her armpits to steady her. Suddenly the drag of the water moved them together and their naked bodies were only inches apart.

Rafael cursed silently. What the hell was he doing here? He knew he should move away—right now—before he did something…they both did something they would seriously regret. But Lottie was still looking at him, torturing him with her steady bold gaze. He felt his traitorous body immediately jerk into action beneath him, trying to rob him of any last self-control.

'Sometimes a challenge isn't there to be won or lost.' Serious now, Lottie's voice was seductively soft. Water was running in rivulets down her face as she tipped it up to meet his, her lips soft and full and maddeningly tempting.

Rafael lowered his head. 'Nevertheless, if this is a challenge I had better warn you it is a very dangerous one.'

'Let's call it something else, then.'

She was so close now, Rafael could see the clumps of dark wet lashes framing her wide eyes.

'More something that has to be confronted.'

Who made that final move? Rafael wasn't sure, but suddenly all resistance gave way to inevitability and their lips were touching. Tentative at first, but with their softness rapidly turning from firm to bruising, from cold damp to searing heat as they plundered each other's mouths without preamble, both taking and giving with equal lack of thought for anything except this one moment, caught up in the forbidden delirium of the kiss.

Their tongues tasted and tangled, their breath hot and gasping as the power of their desire overtook them, dousing all rational thought. With her hands threaded through Rafael's wet curls Lottie pulled him even closer to her, their faces sealed by the damp and by the kiss that was juddering down the length of their seemingly weightless joined bodies beneath them.

Pulling away, Rafael took a gasp of air, peeled their bodies fractionally apart and dragged words from the tiny part of his brain that still had some rational thought.

'Is this what you want, Lottie?' His heart was thumping dangerously fast, and the sight of Lottie's kiss-swollen lips was doing nothing to ease it. 'Because if not you need to say so now—before it's too late.'

Lottie gazed back at him, her eyes heavy with desire, her body aching with an all-consuming need. This *was* what she wanted—what she wanted so badly that she was physically trembling with the power of it, the realisation of it. It didn't make it right, but it made it impossible to resist.

Unable to voice the words, she simply closed the watery gap between them until their bodies met again, moulded against one another in a perfect fit of sexual intimacy.

Rafael let out a guttural growl of raw sexual need and paused for a split second—all it took for that last bit of reason to vanish. Then, sweeping Lottie up in a slippery embrace, he waded towards the end of the pool with her, the water swirling hurriedly out of their way. Splashing up the shallow steps and across the marble tiles, he pushed open the door through to the gym, then strode over to the rubber mat in the middle of the dark room. He half slipped, half fell down on to it with Lottie still in his arms. Locking his elbows, he dug his slippery damp toes down into the mat and straddled Lottie, above her in a press-up position, staring down into her eyes.

This was madness—total madness. But there was something inescapable about it. Since that first second she had walked into his office at the *palazzo* this was all he had wanted to do. To take her, to consume her, to try and fill the yearning chasm that had gripped him ever since she had left.

With the muscles in his biceps rippling, he started to bend his arms as he slowly lowered himself down over her wet and shivering body, his lips seeking hers again, needing the reassurance that this was what she wanted. And she did.

With her cold mouth opening, her lips formed a sexual cavity that longed to be plundered. Rafael gave out a rasping moan and claimed it, his tongue immediately diving into its depths. Then, peeling away, he bent his head, moving his mouth down to her breasts, kissing and licking the soft, wet, chlorine-tasting swell of each one before taking the cold-puckered nipple in his mouth to suck hard, then harder, as he felt Lottie squirm erotically beneath him.

This felt so good. She might not love him, but he could still turn her on—he could still make her body writhe and twitch for him. He gasped when he felt Lottie's hand move down to where he wanted it most, taking his erection in its cold grip, owning his rock-hard length as she moved the skin up and down with trembling fingers.

Her body contorted beneath them, sticking and sucking on the wet mat as she positioned herself for him, ready to be taken. Reluctantly grabbing her hand, he moved it back over his shoulder. He felt her nails dig into his shoulderblades. If this wasn't to be over in a matter of seconds he needed to take control. He slid his own hand down between them, running it over her damply matted pubic hair, slid a finger inside her, parting the warm, soft folds, feeling the tight muscles clench around it as he touched her clitoris and started to rub it with soft but assured pressure.

Hearing her moan, he covered her mouth with his own again, wanting to absorb the energy of her pleasure into his own body, to feel it with her. As she arched her body against his finger he increased the speed until he knew she was almost there. But not quite. Shifting his hips, he replaced his finger with the tip of his penis, then stopped, savouring this second, before sinking his length into her—halfway at first and then, fractionally altering his position, pushing again, more forcefully, until his entire hot, throbbing length was inside her, being gripped mercilessly by her muscles.

With a small yelp Lottie dug her nails into him further as she clung to him feverishly.

'Lottie?' He just about managed to grate out her name as he raised himself up to look into her eyes.

'Don't stop.'

The deep tremble in her voice, together with the faraway look in her eyes that he remembered so well, was all the confirmation he needed.

As she pulled him back down on top of her he felt her muscles tensing and clenching around him, holding him tightly, urging him on. He had to move faster now, increase the rhythm. The want in him was growing and swelling all the time, demanding release. And Lottie matched him, driving him on to join her, to be right there with her when it happened, and he knew that neither of them could hang on much longer.

With no more than five or six deeply penetrating thrusts he felt her body shudder, heard the irregular gasping, panting of her breath and knew that she was there and that he couldn't hold back any longer. A shuddering, squeezing climax surged through his body, so powerful that it seemed to take Lottie with him, and he covered her lips with his own to silence his low, animal growl. As their wet-slicked bodies gripped and convulsed against each other it felt as if the world could end now and neither of them would notice.

CHAPTER EIGHT

BUT THE WORLD hadn't ended. And even before the last shuddering convulsions had left their bodies Rafael was pulling away, looking down at her, the hunger of desire in his eyes turning to a cold watchfulness.

'I'll find us some towels.'

He was up on his feet now, and Lottie watched his naked body as he padded silently across the room, returning with two towels.

'Here.' Handing one to her, he avoided her eyes as she crouched forward to take it and wrap it round her protectively hunched body. 'You mustn't let yourself get cold.'

'No.' He was tying a towel around his waist now. 'Rafe...' Lottie stopped, not sure what she wanted to say but desperate to ward off the chill that couldn't be warmed with a fluffy towel.

'You need to get to bed, Lottie.' He hurried to block any further conversation. 'We both do.'

Everything about his posture, the tone of his voice, the tight line of his mouth, made it quite clear that he was talking about separate beds.

'It's getting very late.'

If she didn't open her eyes it wouldn't be true. Lottie could feel the sunshine streaming in, insistent against her closed lids, making it plain that the next day had dawned whether she liked it or not. That time didn't stop just because of what they had done last night.

Colourful images flickered frame by frame behind her eyes, like an excruciating X-rated home movie. The pool, the gym, the mat...what they had done on the mat... And, worse still, the way Rafael had behaved afterwards.

She had no one to blame except herself. Unfortunately she could remember with bruising clarity the sequence of events, and if it hadn't exactly been totally one-sided she had definitely been the one who'd started it. Maybe she could blame it on her hormones. After what she had been through they had to be all over the place. Or the hypnotic effect of the pool, perhaps. But deep down she knew there was only one thing she could blame it on. The relentless, carnal, erotic effect that Rafael had on her.

And she was only human. There was only so much temptation a woman could take.

She thought back to the image of Rafael at the end of the pool, peeling off his jeans, gloriously naked in the shadows before diving into the water... Sensuous shivers ran through her again. But the temptation had been her undoing, as her screwed-up ball of a heart could testify now.

The sex had been amazing, of course. They had always had the most incredible connection—as if their two bodies had been specifically designed to fit together for the most explosive of results. But last night had felt like something else...as if the lid had been blown off the pressure cooker of their lives, right there and then, in that dark room, on that slippery gym mat. The pain of the past, the strain of the present, the hopes of the future—all detonating in a mushroom cloud of intensely powerful sexual intensity. She could still sense the aftershocks rippling through her.

But it wasn't those memories that were scratching their

nails down her skin now—not the image of his lean, honed body as he'd spread himself on top of her, not the excruciating pleasure when he had pushed inside her, and not even the realisation that no one else could ever, *ever* make love to her like that, make her feel like this.

No. This gash of pain came from what had happened afterwards: the look of distaste on Rafael's face when he had handed her that towel, the way he had almost herded her back up the stairs, watched while she had closed the door of her bedroom, almost as if she was not to be trusted, as if at any moment she might fling herself at him again, force him to make love to her. *That* was what was crucifying her now.

Snapping open her eyes, she pulled back the coverlet and got out of bed. She had to be strong now, not agonise over her mistakes. She would focus on the day ahead, on the reason she was here. The baby—if there was a baby—was the important thing. Wincing slightly, sore where Rafael had been, she took determined strides towards the bathroom.

Rafael was nowhere to be seen when she finally ventured downstairs. Which was a relief. She certainly didn't want to see him. Even if she *had* spent the last hour bracing herself for the awkward meeting, repeatedly going over in her mind how she would be with him: cheerful, light-hearted, casually flippant about what had happened the night before in a *Ho-ho, that was fun, but obviously it didn't mean anything and obviously it won't happen again* sort of way.

But in the event none of her acting skills were needed. Lunch came and went and still there was no sign of him. Several times Lottie passed his study door, pausing gingerly outside to see if she could hear anything. But all was quiet, and she certainly wasn't going to debase herself any further by tapping on his door to see if he was there, looking as if she cared or, worse still, as if she was going to make repugnant demands on him again.

By the evening, when there was still no sign of him, she had convinced herself that he had gone for ever, abandoned her alone in this beautiful place. And she didn't care if he had. In fact it would be for the best. It would save a lot of embarrassment all round.

As twilight started to turn into dusk Lottie decided she needed some fresh air and, pulling on a warm jumper, walked out on to the terrace. There was a full moon tonight, illuminating the garden with a ghostly light, sharpening the outline of the plants and trees so they appeared to be harder, more aggressive versions of their daytime counterparts.

Opening the iron gates, Lottie paused, gazing at the moon's searchlight across the rippled water. It was stunning. Slowly she started to descend the steps to the water, treading carefully through the shadows. The last thing she wanted was to fall now—now that she had been effectively deserted. Heaven knew when anyone would ever find her.

As she neared the bottom she became aware of the sound of an engine and, looking up, saw a speedboat coming towards her, Rafael at the helm. She watched as he came closer; he was standing up, the top half of his body visible above the windscreen, one hand on the wheel, confidently manoeuvring the sleek vessel towards its mooring.

Cutting the engine, he let the boat drift towards the mooring pole and jumped ashore with a rope in his hands.

'What are you doing here?'

It wasn't the warmest of greetings.

'I just was just admiring the view. Across the lake,' she added hurriedly, in case he might have thought *he* was the view.

'Have you eaten?' Pulling the boat towards him, he leant in to retrieve two carrier bags before turning to face her, one in each hand.

'Um, no—not yet.' Lottie stared back at him. Everything about his cold stance suggested that this was a purely practical question rather than a cordial invitation.

'Well, there's plenty of food here.' He shook the bags in his hands. 'I'm going to have to work this evening, so I'll just get a sandwich, but you should make yourself a proper meal.'

'Right.' His uncompromising tone left no room for negotiation, but still Lottie tried. 'If I'm cooking I might as well make something for you too.'

'No, thanks. Like I say, I will just grab a sandwich.'

'Fine.' If he was going to be like that then so be it.

For a moment the two of them faced each other, the moonlight illuminating their profiles, only the slapping sound of the water breaking the silence. Lottie had prepared herself for some awkwardness, but this was more like hostility. She realised that all her fears were founded. She hadn't been mistaken about that look on his face last night. He really did find her repugnant. Up until now she had thought that last night was just a mistake—something that should never have happened. Now she saw it for what it really was—a hideous betrayal, an abhorrent debacle that shamed her to the core.

And everything about the cold, arrogant temperament of the man standing before her now made it quite plain that he thought the same.

Turning away from him, she started to ascend the flight of steps back up to the terrace, furious with herself when hot tears of self-pity started to roll down cheeks already burning with shame and humiliation. She could hear him behind her, taking the steps two at a time, the carrier bags rustling in his hands.

'Lottie, wait.' Catching up, he dropped the bags, putting a hand on her shoulder in an attempt to stop her getting away. 'About last night...'

'Forget it, Rafael.' Shaking him off, she continued to march up the steps, determined that he wasn't going to see her tears. There was certainly no way she was going to talk about it, listen to him telling her that it had been a mistake or, worse still, that he was sorry. That was more than she could bear.

With each step her shame and despair was joined by temper and then anger, until by the time she reached the top she was seething—so much so that she stumbled, falling forward in an ungainly half-trip, half-run that made her heart hammer in her chest.

'Lottie!' A second after his call he was beside her. 'Are you all right?'

'I am fine.' Drawing herself upright, Lottie struggled to regain her balance before she marched off up the terrace path, her defiant words rippling in her wake. 'You really don't need to worry about me.'

Rafael was unpacking the groceries in the kitchen when he realised that Lottie was watching him from the doorway. He looked up quickly, registering the flush of her cheeks, the halo of hair, full of static from the woollen jumper she had just pulled over her head, the rise and fall of her breasts beneath the tight fabric of the tee shirt beneath. She looked both sexy and vulnerable. But, more than that, she looked as if she was fighting to hold in a lot of things she was desperate to say.

'I'll be out of your way in a minute.'

This produced nothing more than a shrug of her shoulders.

'I've bought some prosciutto and fresh pasta, and there are plenty of vegetables or salad if you would prefer.' He shut the fridge door and leant against it.

'Thanks.'

She had swept into the room now and brushed past him to fill the kettle. The air was full of the floral scent of hostility.

'Look, Lottie, if this is about last night...'

'Last night?' She flashed him a contemptuous stare. 'Did anything happen last night?'

'There is no point in being childish.'

His patience was wearing thin now. He was tired from lack of sleep and the long and tedious telephone conference that he had had to take away from the villa because of her. He was hungry, and he was furious with himself for letting last night happen.

'I think we have to acknowledge the foolishness of what we did and ensure that we don't find ourselves in that position again.'

The ice in Lottie's cold blue eyes almost froze the words in his throat.

'I'm sure we both regret it now.'

He certainly did. Even though he had been twitching to make love to Lottie for weeks now. Even though every little thing she said or did set him off, and even though there had been countless times when he had wanted to pull her to him, feel the luscious softness of her against him, rip off her clothes, claim her naked body for his own—any or all of the above. But he had been convinced he could handle his infatuation, he really had. A master of control, it was inconceivable that he would give in to his weakness.

When they had been at the *palazzo* it hadn't been quite

so difficult. With the pressure of work and meetings and business trips—not all of which had been strictly necessary—he had been able to keep out of her way, distract himself enough with the hundred and one things that needed his attention. Plus the place was big enough to hide in. Though the thought that *he*, the Conte di Monterrato, respected head of the principality, formidable businessman, someone who had never run away from anything in his life before, should be hiding himself away from this young woman—a woman he had vowed never to let get to him again—held an irony that wasn't lost on him.

But in the villa there was no escaping her. It shocked him, this visceral effect she had on him. It almost knocked the breath out of him and he needed all his powers of self-control to keep up the façade of indifference, to stop the mask from slipping and revealing the unadulterated lust beneath. Now he knew all his pretence had been for nothing and he had been shown to be the fool he really was—a fool for exposing himself again to the woman who had broken his heart and a fool for ever thinking he could resist her.

As if to drive home the point Lottie moved past him again, turning her back on him and bending down to take a saucepan out of the cupboard. He stared at the pale strip of skin above the low waistband of her jeans, at the way the denim stretched tautly over her pert behind. *Dio!*

'Well, that's nice to know.' Banging the saucepan down onto the hob, Lottie reached across for the kettle and recklessly sloshed in water. 'Thank you for enlightening me about how I feel. For telling me that I regret it every bit as much as you do. That makes me feel so much better.'

'Lottie…' Rafael reached for her arm but she backed away from him with the agility of a springbok.

'Don't touch me, Rafael. Don't come anywhere near me.

Last night was a mistake. You have made that perfectly clear. Now, if you would like to get out of the kitchen, I would like to prepare my meal in peace.'

Picking up a knife, she sliced at the plastic film of a container and shook pasta into the pan. 'The meal I will be eating alone, because you are *too busy* to join me.'

'I am just saying, Lottie, that after last night it is probably best if we give each other some space.' Rafael raked an exasperated hand through his tangle of dark curls.

'Well, what are you waiting for?' Lottie gestured towards the door with the knife. 'There is plenty of space out there.'

'If I have upset you then…'

'Don't you *dare*.' Lottie's blue eyes flashed from cold to fire with murderous intent. 'Don't you dare tell me that you are sorry.'

Watching the computer screen close down in front of him, Rafael leaned back in his chair. He should have had more than enough work to keep his mind occupied—apart from anything else he was hosting a charity dinner in a week's time, a fundraising event for the premature baby foundation he had set up in his daughter's name. But despite staring at spreadsheets and banging out emails for a couple of hours the tension of his confrontation with Lottie had still refused to lessen.

Using his foot, he pushed himself away from the desk and stood up, stretching the bunched muscles of his arms out before him.

What made this so unbearable—what made his mood black enough to block out the moon—was this feeling of loss of control. He had lost it last night—spectacularly so. Given in to his carnal instincts. No, more than that, he had given in to Lottie herself. And it pained him to recognise that that meant so much more than just sex.

Despite his best efforts to regain control this evening all he had done was make things worse. His bad-mannered behaviour had simply stirred up the simmering cauldron of unspoken tension and newly raw feelings.

All of which made him want to go out and kick something. *Hard.* Made him want to go out and do something that would put him in extreme danger. Because that was what he did when he felt like this. An adrenaline junkie, he needed his fix—it was the only thing that went half-way to easing his pain.

But not this time. Risking his life was not the answer—he could see that now. He had to face up to the reality of the situation and deal with it. From tomorrow there were six more days to get through here in the villa—surely he could do that? If playing happy families wasn't going to work he would have to come up with some other strategy.

Six more days until they could do the pregnancy test, find out what their future held.

Moving over to the window, he stared through his troubled reflection to the quiet dark of the night. If the test was positive...well, they would obviously have to work out how they were going to proceed. But the joy of knowing he was going to be a father would more than compensate for any difficult decisions. And if it was negative...

Pressing his forehead against the cool glass, Rafael felt the cruel fingers of doubt squeeze at his heart. If it was negative not only would he have lost his only chance of having a child, he would also have lost Lottie.

Turning away, he picked up a couple of files from the desk and, tucking them under his arm, headed for the door.

There was no doubt that if there was no baby then Lottie would disappear from his life for ever.

Cursing himself for even caring, Rafael slammed the door behind him.

CHAPTER NINE

Lottie found the note when she came downstairs, propped up against the coffee machine.

Urgent business in Milan. Back tomorrow. Contactable by mobile, any time.

Holding the piece of paper in her hands, she stared at the familiar handwriting. She could almost feel the chill coming off the page, the frostbite in the words. So he had gone, then. They only had two nights left in the villa but he hadn't been able to stay, to put up with being around her any longer. She didn't believe for one moment that it was business, urgent or not, that had taken him away. It was *her* he wanted to get away from. Everything about his behaviour over the past few days had made that perfectly clear.

Cold didn't begin to describe it. A polar vortex was more like it—a chill factor of minus thirty whenever they came across one another…something that had happened less and less as the days had gone on. Rafael would be working in his study or punishing himself down in the gym while Lottie spent her time upstairs painting, all the time listening for the sound of Rafael's footsteps to make sure she wouldn't have to meet him on the stairs, or share the kitchen with him when they both hurried in to make some hastily prepared food before disappearing again to eat alone.

Lottie felt bad enough about what they had done—the Big Mistake. She was furious with herself for the way she had behaved, for inviting Rafael into the pool with her, for making it so obvious just how much she wanted him. The image of them on that mat simply refused to go away: the raw animal sex, the way she had clung to him like a half-starved waif, clawing at him, urging him on, desperate to bring him to orgasm with her, to share that ultimate sexual intensity. She had gone over it in her head a thousand times but she was still no closer to understanding how it had happened.

But it had, and now her fury wasn't just limited to herself. It had spread, like a bush fire, to encompass Rafael as well. Okay, so maybe she had started it, but she wasn't going to take responsibility for the whole debacle. If Rafael found her so distasteful—as his behaviour over the past few days clearly showed he did—why the hell had he succumbed to her, made love to her? No—correction—why had he had sex with her in that fiercely passionate way? Had the thought of sex just been too tempting? Even sex with someone as offensive as her? Because if that was the case that was *his* problem. It certainly didn't give him the right to treat her the way he had these past few days.

Filling the kettle, Lottie sat on a barstool, watching the water starting to bubble through the plastic panel.

Beneath the anger lurked another emotion: sadness. Sadness that she and Rafael couldn't even spend two weeks in each other's company without it descending into this. No matter what silly hopes she might have harboured that they would be able to get on, be normal together—be friends, even—that was exactly what those hopes had been: silly.

Or, to put it another way, downright ridiculously stupid. And as for them being parents...

Dropping a teabag into her mug, she doused it with water. She couldn't begin to face that problem yet. She might never have to, of course. And that, in itself, would bring an anguish all of its own that she refused to think about now. Squeezing the life out of the teabag, she dropped it into the metal bin with a clang.

For now she would concentrate on the positive. She had twenty-four hours to herself—twenty-four hours when she could breathe normally, without the constant shadow of Rafael being around to torment her. She decided she would make the most of the time—starting with a solid day's painting. Channelling her pent-up energies into something creative seemed like the best idea.

Picking up the note for one last look, Lottie screwed it into a ball and dropped it into the bin before heading upstairs with her tea.

The next day arrived, clear and blue. Day fourteen. The day that would alter the whole course of her life. Without Rafael around Lottie had slept surprisingly well and now, up and dressed, she was already on her third cup of de-caffeinated coffee.

She had had a good look at her body in the shower that morning, sure that if she really was pregnant it would have to show somewhere. She knew that sore boobs were one of the first signs, so she had paid particular attention to soaping them under the pummelling of the water, desperately trying to convince herself that they were more tender than usual. By the time she had finished they had felt a little different—but then so would any part of her body that had been mercilessly scrubbed for five minutes. The fact was there were no signs; she had absolutely no idea if she was pregnant or not.

Now she fiddled with the mobile phone in her hand. There had been no messages from Rafael. But why would there be—even if she had been obsessively checking for the past hour? No doubt he had enjoyed his night of freedom as much as her. Why would he spoil the relief of not being around her by bothering to text her?

Not for the first time she found herself imagining what he had done last night, her tortured mind immediately flinging him into the arms of some exotically beautiful woman who would be only too happy to soothe his scarred brow, give him a night of pleasure to take his mind off his troubles. She forced herself to stop right there. This day was going to be momentous enough without chucking in any unnecessary masochism.

She realised that she had no idea what time Rafael would be back, and she certainly wasn't going to give him the satisfaction of asking. Absently feeling the weight of her phone, she considered what to do. He might well be on his way now, but she was damned if she was going to be sitting here waiting for him. No. Her decision was made— she was going to go out and buy a pregnancy testing kit.

The very thought of it made her shiver, every nerve-ending zinging with excitement and anticipation and fear. With a shaky hand she started to look up the number of a local taxi firm to take her into the nearest town. But then she stopped. She had a better idea.

The villa was deserted when Rafael arrived back later that day. He could sense the silence as soon as he strode in, even before he had checked the downstairs rooms and started pounding up the stairs, two at a time. Pushing open the first door, he could smell the oil paint and turpentine as he gazed about him, taking in the large canvas that was on an easel in the middle of the room, the vibrant colours of an evening sunset vividly portrayed by Lottie's unmistakable sweeping brushstrokes.

But no Lottie.

Turning, he felt his heart-rate increase as a terrible thought took hold. He marched across the landing to her bedroom, his eyes raking over the untidy room, searching for clues. Going over to her wardrobe, he flung open the doors; there were her clothes, swinging gently on their hangers, a small pile of shoes scattered beneath.

Breathing heavily, he went and sat down on the edge of her bed, relief pulsing through his veins. *Grazie a Dio.* She was still here, then. He glanced down at her bedside table. There was the book she was reading, opened facedown, its spine cracking, along with a jumble of bracelets, some make-up, a lipstick. Picking up the latter, Rafael felt it between his fingers, removing the top and twisting it to reveal the raspberry-red colour. She had been wearing this the night they had gone out for that meal. The same night they had ended up having passionate sex on a wet gym mat.

He ran his hand over his eyes at the memory of the appalling way he had behaved. But as he looked around at the unmade bed, the rumpled sheets, the indentation on the pillow where her head had been, he knew that Lottie was like a forbidden substance to him. She got to him in a way that no other woman ever could. He didn't know why, and much as he had tried to figure it out, tried to deny it to himself, he now realised it was just an irrefutable, indisputable fact.

But where the hell was she? Initial relief gave way to another wave of anxiety. Supposing she had already done a pregnancy test and it had proved negative. Had she taken herself off somewhere to lick her wounds? Was that why she had disappeared?

Rafael knew just how much Lottie wanted this baby. He thought back to when they had discussed it—when she had tried to explain about her deep-rooted desire to be a mother, about wanting to do right all the things her own mother had done wrong.

And how had he reacted? With compassion and understanding? Or even with relief that here was a young woman who knew her own mind, who was doing it for herself, not as some sort of twisted favour to him? No, he hadn't reacted in any of those ways. He had bitten her head off, snarled at her about how he had feelings too. He could still see the look of hurt in her eyes before he had turned away. What he didn't know was when he had turned into such a bastard.

Marching down the corridor, he checked his phone yet again, to see if she had answered his messages. He could feel anger surging through him now, pushing the anxiety to one side. It was an emotion he was far more comfortable with, if he was honest. Jabbing at her number, he cursed when, after a few rings, it went to voicemail. He heard himself bark, 'Where the hell are you?' before returning the phone to his pocket and thundering out onto the terrace.

Scanning the sun-rippled lake, he watched the traffic of assorted boats weaving about on the water. With no particular plan in mind, he started to descend the steps to the water's edge, stopping with a jolt and a thudding heart halfway down. The speedboat had gone. Fear gripped his heart and a hundred different scenarios ran through his mind, each one worse than the last.

What had happened here? Whatever had possessed him to leave her alone last night? How in the name of God could he have been so selfish?

With panic and fear wrestling in his chest, clawing at his throat, he ran down the remaining steps, pulling the phone out of his pocket, punching in the number for his security team, already visualising the ransom demands, the terrifying danger Lottie could be in.

A loud toot made him look up. A speedboat—*his* speedboat—was heading towards him, with Lottie at the wheel, waving casually. What the—? A new, but nonetheless urgent anxiety gripped Rafael; she was going far too fast, she was using only one hand, and she was heading straight for the moorings.

'Slow down!' Cupping his hands over his mouth, he screamed at her over the roar of the engine. 'Cut the engine!'

The boat did an erratic zig-zag as Lottie stood up to try and hear what he was saying.

'Cut the engine!'

Finally comprehending, Lottie gave him an okay sign and the throaty roar stopped. But the momentum of its speed was still carrying the boat far too fast as it cut through the water towards him.

'Sideways on!'

He could see Lottie clearly now, cheeks flushed with the fresh air, blonde hair streaming out behind her. At least she had both hands on the wheel now.

'Turn!' Indicating with wildly flailing arms, he tried to get her to understand what to do. 'Turn the wheel. Come in sideways!'

There was a crunch, followed by a long scraping sound, followed by a delicate, 'Oops...'

Unscrewing his eyes, he saw his speedboat now indignantly at rest against the far end of the dock. And Lottie, wobbling as she tried to stand, calmly getting ready to disembark.

'*Mio Dio!*' He was beside her in a flash, extending an arm to help her ashore. 'Are you hurt?'

'No, of course not.' Refusing to make eye contact, Lottie let go of his hand the second she was on dry land. 'I'm not quite so sure about the boat, though, I'm afraid there might be a bit of a scrape…'

As she turned back to look at it Rafe caught hold of her arm, spinning her round to face him.

'I don't give a damn about the boat.' He glared down at her, his voice harsh with immense relief. 'What the hell do you think you were doing? You don't have the first idea how to drive that thing. You could have killed yourself.'

'Well, I didn't.' Shaking her elbow free, Lottie defiantly glared back at him. 'And for your information I actually managed perfectly fine until you started interfering.'

'Right.' Rafael matched her stare. 'So it's *my* fault, is it? My fault that you were hurtling towards the shore at sixty knots per hour?'

'Yes—yes, it was.' Lottie wasn't going to back down. 'You made me lose my concentration.'

'Well, all I can say is it's a good job I did. Your "concentration" was going to end up taking you to the bottom of the lake—along with a pile of fibreglass that had once been my boat.'

'Don't exaggerate.' Tossing her head, Lottie turned to retrieve her bag from the seat of the damaged boat.

'Where have you been, anyway?'

'Just to do a little shopping.'

'Why didn't you answer my calls?'

Retrieving her phone from the bag, Lottie registered the seven missed calls. 'I was driving, remember? Surely you know you shouldn't use your phone when you are driving?'

She raised her eyebrows at him, all too aware, but not caring in the least, that she was seriously winding him up.

'So, where *is* this shopping?' Not that it mattered. But, needing the distraction, Rafael looked around and could see no evidence of it.

'Here.'

Their eyes met over the chemist's bag that Lottie slowly withdrew from her handbag and the world around them suddenly skidded to a halt.

'Ah. I see.'

Silence hung heavily between them.

'You are going to do it now?' His voice seemed to come from a long way away, his eyes remaining fixed on the unremarkable bag.

Lottie nodded. 'I guess so.' She gave a throwaway laugh. 'Now's as good a time as any.'

There was another brief silence.

'*Buono.*'

Brisk now, businesslike, Rafael took a step towards her and attempted to put an arm around her shoulder. But Lottie refused to respond and it ended up more like a manly pat on the back. Awkwardness pushed them apart again.

'Come on, then.' Clearing his throat, he tried again. 'Let's do this.'

Rafael was standing by the window, his back to her, when Lottie emerged from the bathroom. She was delicately holding the tester stick in front of her, as if it was made of plutonium, or something capable of destroying their lives.

'How long?' Turning, Rafael looked at her, then at it, the catch in his voice betraying his tension along with his shoulders, which were hitched unnaturally high.

'It says up to three minutes.'

Lottie could barely speak. Sinking down on the bed,

she tried to regulate her breathing—to breathe at all, in fact. She felt dizzy, her hands shaky and clammy as they gripped the plastic time bomb.

Crossing over to the bed, Rafael gently took the tester stick from her and placed it face-down on the table. He squatted beside her, taking her hands between his own, his warm strength pumping into her.

'I want to say something to you, Lottie.'

Lottie didn't want to hear it—not now, not ever, actually. She couldn't face any more emotional trauma. This waiting was threatening to kill her, *literally*. She realised she couldn't breathe any more and the room was starting to spin.

'Lottie.' Giving her hands a shake, Rafael halted her panic attack enough to make her suck in a breath and look at him. 'I want to say thank you for doing this.'

'There's no need…'

'Yes—yes, there is. Whatever the outcome, I truly appreciate that you were prepared to at least try to give me my last chance of being a father.'

Why was he talking like this? As if he already knew the result was going to be negative? He who had always been so convinced that this time it would work. Did he know something she didn't?

Lottie looked at him with fear in her eyes.

'I know this is the last thing you expected when I asked you to come to Palazzo Monterrato. That you actually thought you had come to sign divorce papers.' A tightness pulled at the corners of his mouth as he spoke. 'And if there is no baby you will, of course, have your wish. I will put divorce proceedings into place straight away and you will have your freedom. But either way I want you to know you have my heartfelt thanks.'

Well, thanks to that little speech Lottie now felt a whole

lot worse. As she looked into the shadowed depths of his eyes she wondered yet again how everything between them had managed to go so horribly wrong. How something that had started with such love and passion and hope and excitement had ended up with her sitting here, on the edge of a bed, waiting to find out if she was pregnant by a man who didn't love her, in the hope of having a child that they would never be able to parent together. Not in the true sense of the word, anyway.

The last thing she wanted was his *heartfelt thanks* or, worse still, her freedom. Suddenly she knew what she wanted him to say more than anything in the world. She wanted him to say that everything would be all right— that no matter whether she was pregnant or not he loved her and that was enough. That they could build a future together, be a couple, have a happy life, grow old together.

She forced out a slow, deliberate breath. The thought that that thing, just inches away from her, held not only her fate but also her heart in its little plastic window was almost more than she could bear.

Speech done, Rafael released her hands and stood up. Then, looking at his watch, he raised his eyebrows at her.

'No.' Lottie's hands were trembling so badly she couldn't have picked it up if she'd tried. Her stomach was heaving as if she was going to be sick. 'I can't do it.'

'You want me to?'

Lottie nodded, watching in horrified slow motion as his arm stretched across to pick up the tester stick, registering the rolled-up sleeve, the tanned forearm, the strong, purposeful hand raising it, turning it over. Then she screwed her eyes shut.

For a second there was nothing but blind silence.

'Well?' She heard her unrecognisable voice squeak the question.

Still nothing.

She opened her eyes. There was Rafael, still in front of her, still holding the tester stick in his hand. His expression was—what? Blank? Stunned? With a sickening plummet of dread, Lottie suddenly realised that his eyes were shining with the gleam of tears.

Oh, God. Oh, no.

'It's positive, Lottie.' His gaze swept from the stick in his hand to her incredulous face, his own face a picture of wonder and awe. 'We are going to have a baby.'

The restaurant was full, couples at every table, with candles and roses and love in the air. As they were shown to their table by a deferential waiter Lottie realised what day it was: San Valentino—Valentine's Day. And just for tonight Lottie was going to let herself join in, soak up the atmosphere, be part of it. She was with the most handsome man in the restaurant, probably on the planet, as several female glances following their entrance confirmed, she was in the most euphoric bubble of happiness, and she was pregnant.

Yes, sirree, definitely pregnant. Both the tester kits she had bought had proved positive, and one of them was still nestling unhygienically in her handbag—as if throwing it away might suddenly make her *un*pregnant again.

She had never seen Rafael looking like this before. An inner happiness was shining through him, radiating from him. At first glance a stranger might not have noticed the difference, just seen the same stunningly handsome man as before—it wasn't as if he was grinning from ear to ear or slapping people on the back and buying them drinks. But Lottie could see it, and that made it all the more special.

She hugged the realisation to her chest that *she* was responsible for this, *she* was the one who had brought about this change in him. She could have gazed at him all night—

he looked so totally, utterly beautiful. But obviously she wouldn't do that because that would be weird. And besides she was hungry—starving, in fact.

A bottle of pink champagne appeared at their table, and after pouring them both a glass Rafael raised his, waiting for Lottie to do the same.

'*Buon San Valentino.*'

'Thank you. And Happy Valentine's Day to you too.' They clinked glasses and Lottie looked into the happy bubbles. 'But perhaps I had better not.'

'I'm sure half a glass won't hurt. Besides, you have to drink pink champagne on Valentine's Day. It's the law.'

'Is that right?' Taking a couple of delicate sips, Lottie let the dry fizz slip down her throat.

This was what happiness was—this little capsule that they were in now...her, Rafael and the impending baby. Even though she knew that things were going to be difficult, that she and Rafael faced all sorts of challenges with the baby and with their relationship, she refused to think about that now. This evening she was going to allow herself to be unquestioningly, unreservedly happy.

Raising her head, she realised that Rafael was studying her, his head tilted to one side, the champagne glass still in his hand. She looked down again, for some reason feeling shy, worried that he might be able to read her mind, but he reached across the table for her hand, covering it with his own.

'What were you thinking?'

Phew. Obviously he was lacking that particular superpower.

'Nothing.' Nothing she was going to tell him. He was big-headed enough as it was.

'Happy?'

'Yes.' She looked at him solemnly. 'You?'

'More than you could ever believe. Thank you, Lottie.'

'That's okay. I didn't exactly get pregnant all on my own, you know.'

'True. I suppose I should be a bit proud of myself too.'

'I was talking about Dr Oveisi.' Her eyes flashed mischievously.

'That is cruel, young lady, and you know it.' He shot her a heart-melting glance. 'Now, start being nice to me or I will call that violinist over and make him play for you all night.'

'Don't you dare.' Rafael knew all too well that she found those things toe-curlingly embarrassing. 'From now on I promise to be sweetness and light.'

They ate artichokes and roasted sea bass, shared forks full of food and light-hearted chatter, and all the time the sensual sexual chemistry fizzed between them just as it always did whenever they were together. Only this time it went unchecked, insidiously binding them with its invisible threads, pulling them closer and closer together.

They smiled at each other, teased and flirted, pulled faces over the sharp coldness of the lemon *gelato*, drank tiny cups of bitter coffee, then finally left arm in arm to stroll back to the wounded speedboat for the short journey back to the villa.

'Warm enough?' As the boat hummed quietly through the water Rafael looked across at Lottie.

'Yes, fine.' The night air was prickly with cold but she was wearing Rafael's thick woollen coat, cosily tucked in, loving the scent of him that was coming off it. 'Look at all those stars.'

Throwing back her head, she watched as they passed overhead—thousands and thousands of them. They made her feel brave, somehow, as if what they were doing was right, part of the future, part of a wider scheme of things.

Returning her gaze to the front, she realised Rafael was looking at her.

'Oi—keep your eyes on the water, you.'

'I hardly think you are in a position to tell me how to drive this boat.' Grinning, Rafael faced forward again. 'The poor thing is still bearing the scars of your little outing. Very expensive scars too, I might add.'

'Yeah, sorry about that. I suppose I *was* going a bit fast.'

'Totally out of control, more like it. Allow me to show you how it should be done.' He pulled down the throttle to no more than a gentle hum and the boat slowed down immediately. Rafael guided it perfectly alongside the mooring pole.

'Show-off.'

Rafael shrugged his shoulders immodestly. Leaping out of the boat, he secured it to the mooring pole and then held out a hand to Lottie.

This evening had been so perfect she realised she didn't want it to end. As they climbed the steps, walked along the terrace pathway and into the villa, she felt as if she were in a fragile fairytale—one that might turn into pumpkins and rats at any moment if she wasn't careful.

Once inside, Rafe removed his coat from her shoulders. 'Drink?'

'A cup of tea would be nice.'

'It shall be yours.'

Lottie sat on the window seat, gazing out over the lake. *Pregnant.* She could hardly believe it. And although she knew she shouldn't jinx it, something inside her—some inner sense—told her that this time everything was going to be all right.

A rattling tray announced Rafael's return, and after carefully placing a cup of tea in front of Lottie he removed his own tumbler of whisky and came and sat beside her on the sofa. Lottie realised he had something in his other hand.

'I bought you this.' His voice was low, almost gruff, as he opened his hand to reveal the 'something'. It was a small blue velvet box.

Lottie looked from the box to Rafael, her eyes questioning.

'Thank you.' Surprised, she wasn't sure what to say. 'I'm afraid I don't have anything for you.'

Rafael frowned at her, puzzled. 'Why would you?'

'Well, I'm assuming this is a Valentine's Day gift?'

'Hardly!' He all but snorted. 'I just happened to see them and thought you might like them.' Handing her the closed box, he pulled back. 'Think of them as a token of my gratitude, if you like.'

'Right...' That had told her. Gratitude was as good as it was going to get.

Opening the box revealed a pair of gold and enamel earrings shaped like little violets, their perfect petals shaded to a deep purple in the centre, where a small, gold nugget nestled.

'They are beautiful!' With one in each hand Lottie held them before her.

'I'm glad you like them. I thought the colour was pretty, that they would go with your eyes...' His voice trailed off.

'I love them. Thank you.'

'Are you going to try them on?'

'Yes, of course.' But he was too close, watching her too intently, and in spite of fiddling with her earlobes Lottie couldn't get them to go in. 'I need a mirror, really.'

'Here—let me.' Squatting before her, Rafael took the earrings out of her hand and proceeded very delicately to fix first one, then the other to her ears. Feeling his breath blowing sweetly against her cheeks, Lottie found herself painfully holding in her own.

'There.' Job done, he sat back on his heels.

Touching her earlobes, Lottie looked into his face. 'Thank you.'

She leant forward, intending to give him a polite kiss on the cheek, but he intercepted her, catching her face in his hands. Their eyes clashed. Her heart thudded wildly.

For a second neither moved, each trying to gauge the other's reaction. Then Lottie, realising that she had no idea how to read the mind of the man who crouched before her, gave up.

To hell with it. This was her night to do what *she* wanted. And what she wanted more than anything else was Rafael. As she gazed into his beautiful face she had never felt more sure of anything in her whole life. The joy of knowing she was pregnant with his baby was almost overwhelming her body with happiness and pride. But there was one more thing that could make this day absolutely perfect. And it was right in front of her now.

Linking her hands behind Rafael's neck, she pulled him the few inches closer she needed to bring his lips to hers. Rafael let go of her face, but instead of mirroring her action his arms fell by his sides. Undeterred, Lottie pressed her mouth against his, her lips already pouting and swollen, her fingers threading through his hair, pulling him closer to increase the pressure.

Still Rafael resisted, but when she opened her mouth, slid her tongue between his lips, gently plundered inside, she could feel his stubbornness evaporate as he started to return the kiss in the way only he could—with fire and deep passion. It sent a shudder of pure craving through her body.

Coming off his haunches, he wrapped his arms around her, pulling her up with him as they wobbled to stand, each clinging unsteadily to the other, desperate to find each other's lips again. Pressed so tightly to him, Lottie revelled in the heat coming off his body, in the feel of his muscular arms imprisoning her against his granite chest, the thrilling evidence of his arousal, hard and insistent against her pelvis.

And tonight of all nights there was no way this could be resisted.

As if both were under the same crazy spell they started to tug at each other's clothes.

Lottie pulled roughly at the buttons of his shirt sliding her hands inside, across the muscular planes of his chest, the hair coarse beneath her fingertips, his nipples tightening under her touch. Slipping the shirt over his shoulders, she started on his suit trousers, pulling down the zipper and easing them over his hips. They pooled on the floor around his ankles, revealing the straining boxer shorts. *Oh, yes!* She ran her hand over the huge swell of his member, which was trying to force its way free, and felt him clench beneath her touch.

Rafael moved away fractionally, standing on one leg and then the other to rip off his socks and kick the pile of discarded clothes to one side. Then he turned his attention to Lottie, gripping her shoulders and spinning her around. With trembling hands he lowered the zipper of her dress, peeling it open to expose the satin-smooth sweep of her back, the neat curve of her waistline, the pert roundness of her bottom beneath skimpy white panties. He let the dress slither to the floor and turned Lottie to face him again.

She looked so damned hot, standing there, her chin raised in some sort of defiance, wearing nothing but a bra and panties, with a violet flash in her eyes that said not so much *Take me* as *I challenge you not to take me*—a challenge that Rafael already knew he had lost.

Stepping forward, he lowered his head to the level of her breasts, trailing light kisses over the softness of the flesh above her bra before homing in on the channel of cleavage, plundering it with his tongue.

Lottie gripped at his hair, pulling him closer, the touch of his lips on her breasts sending waves of exquisite pleasure through her body. She wanted more. *Now.*

Unfastening her bra, Rafe let it fall to the ground between them as he cupped her breasts, first one and then the other, pushing them upwards so he could take her nipples in his mouth, his hot breath shrinking them to shrivelled peaks of longing even before his lips had circled them, his teeth had grazed their hardness.

He let his tongue trail down her chest, feeling her stomach muscles clenching violently as he passed her tummy button and reached the top of her panties. Moving a hand to either side of her hips, he yanked them down with a single movement and cast them to one side. Then, putting his hands back on her hips, he shifted sideways until he was in the perfect position to slide his tongue inside her.

She was so wet. Her body was such a giveaway it was almost embarrassing. If she had wanted to play it cool, pretend in any way that she could take him or leave him, she'd have had no chance. Rafael only had to touch her, initiate the very first moment of lovemaking, and her body started screaming at him to take her. Now she was standing there so turned on she was literally trembling, arching her body to increase the pressure of his tongue against her, her head thrown back with indecent abandon, her fingers buried and tugging at his hair as his tongue increased in pressure, sending spasms of yearning pleasure shooting through her.

As the first shudders of orgasm started to roll through her she felt him stop, come up to a standing position, rip off his boxer shorts and press the steel rod of his erection hard against her stomach.

'No, *cara*...' Rafael's voice was a deep sexy whisper. 'Not yet.'

Scooping her off her feet, he crossed the few steps to the sofa, laying her down, ready to cover her body with his own. But, sliding across, Lottie made room for him beside her, before quickly wriggling on top of him. She wanted to do it *her* way this time. And as she looked down into his eyes she could see that he had no intention of stopping her.

Pure, unadulterated desire flashed between them. An unstoppable force.

Spreading her legs, she reached for his throbbing shaft, holding it against the tight, warm wetness of her need. With a low moan she felt Rafael shift beneath her and the tip of his penis enter her. She shivered erotically. She needed him inside her now—the whole of him, not just the swell of the tip but his entire length, thrust deep, deep inside her.

And that was what happened. With a gasp of pleasure she felt him plunge into her, her muscles clenching round him, intense pleasure shooting though her. Gripping on to her hips, his strong hands held her steady for a second, but she was desperate to feel him even more deeply and, leaning back, she ground her hips into his and started to move.

Matching her bucking thrusts with his own, he increased the pace all the time, along with the total ecstasy, until she was totally lost in it, only dimly aware of Rafael's hoarsely whispered words.

'Not yet, *cara,* keep it going…you can do this…a bit more, a bit more, a bit…'

Finally the words stopped as she fell down on top of him and felt the violent orgasm rack through his body, taking her with it in an amazing, overwhelming crescendo.

CHAPTER TEN

WHEN LOTTIE WOKE the next morning she was in Rafael's bed with Rafael beside her, propped on one elbow, looking down at her with those beautiful brown eyes.

'*Buongiorno.*'

'Good morning.' She snuggled towards him, tipping her profile up, the little violet earring digging into the skin behind her ear.

Sweeping a twisted strand of fair hair away from her eyes, Rafael bent to place a light, almost polite kiss on her lips. 'Did you sleep well'?

'Mmm…very well, thank you.'

Raising her arms, she pulled him back down under the covers, curling her naked body against his. Spending the night in the same bed as him had felt so right. Especially after what they had done together last night.

'How are you feeling this morning?' Despite the innocent question she could feel the temptation in him.

'Pregnant.' The word was muffled against the warm skin of his neck. She felt him nudge against her, trying to move her position so that he could see her face, but she resisted, smiling to herself in her dark, sensuous, happy place.

'Really?' He adjusted his position so that his chin was now resting on the top of her head. 'Do you actually feel any different?'

Different? The word was too bland to describe the total change of Lottie's state of mind. After the tension of being imprisoned in the villa with Rafael, the hurt and anger of the past few days, the terrible gripping anxiety of the pregnancy test, she now felt free, relaxed, euphoric—as if suddenly everything was going to be all right. The massive weight she had been carrying around, even if she had largely refused to acknowledge it, had been lifted, and now she could float with happiness. And judging by the feel of Rafael beside her now, the completely different mood they shared this morning, it was exactly the same for him

'No, not different in that way.' She tipped her head up to answer his question. 'I meant pregnant as in that was my first thought when I woke up.' She smiled at him. 'The realisation that it really is true.'

Rafael stared down at her, his deep brown eyes glowing softly. 'I know. It's amazing, isn't it? *Sorprendente.* But we do have nine months to get used to the idea.'

'Yes.' Lottie returned his gaze, her own eyes dancing indigo blue. 'Aren't we lucky?'

'Yes. We are.' His hand slid under the covers and found her flat tummy, running over it in a gentle smoothing motion. She knew he was thinking about the baby, but her thoughts were turning in a very different direction.

'I guess we should get up.'

'You're right.'

His hand slid lower, and lower still, until it found the place she'd so much hoped it would. Maybe he wasn't thinking about the baby after all.

'Do we really have to go back to the *palazzo*?' She arched her back, brushing her breasts against him. 'Can't we just stay here for ever?'

'Nice try.' He reciprocated by moving his finger lightly

against her. 'But I have a stack of business to attend to. Not to mention a charity dinner to oversee.' His voice was becoming increasingly guttural.

'Hmm, we'd better get going, then.' Taking her own hand down under the cover now, she watched as his eyes widened.

'I couldn't agree more, Contessa Revaldi.'

Holding her shoulders, Rafael slid underneath her, transferring his hands to her hips so that he positioned her perfectly on top of him.

'But first there is a little business here that I need to attend to.'

'I see what you mean.' Lottie squirmed on top of him. 'And not all that little…'

The helicopter ride back to Palazzo Monterrato seemed to take no time at all—which was just as well, given that their morning in bed had somehow turned to afternoon and dusk was already falling when Rafael expertly landed the noisy machine on the helipad.

Lottie watched as he flicked off the controls, removing his headset and seatbelt, then turned to wait for her to do the same. It was stupid, but she was reluctant to get out. She would have liked their journey to go on for ever, to be cocooned in the glass bubble of happiness that she'd shared with her handsome pilot. But end it had, and as they walked up the long driveway towards the *palazzo* Rafael cleared his throat, obviously building up to saying something.

'So, about this charity dinner…' He stared straight ahead as he strode beside her. 'Obviously I want everything to go perfectly.'

'Charity dinner?' Lottie turned to look at him. 'What charity dinner?'

'The one I told you about earlier.'

Lottie frowned, trying to recall. 'I don't remember. When is it?'

'Tomorrow.'

'Tomorrow? Here at the *palazzo*?'

'Of course.'

She waited, but no more information was forthcoming, the only sound coming from the gravel that crunched beneath their feet.

'So what are you saying? That you want me to make myself scarce?'

'Why would I want you to do that?' He glanced at her quickly before fixing his gaze straight ahead again.

'I don't know.' Suddenly unsure of herself, Lottie faltered.

'What I would like is for you to play the role of hostess.'

'Oh.' She hated these things, and the unfriendly way he was suggesting it didn't make it any more appealing. 'Are you sure? Won't people think it a bit odd—I don't know—get the wrong impression about us.'

'I don't give a damn about what people think.' Rafael's tone went from cold to harsh. 'And I said *play the role*, Lottie. It's not as if I am expecting you to actually believe in it. I merely feel it would be fitting to have you by my side for the evening.' He came to an abrupt halt outside the villa. 'Especially in view of the charity concerned.'

'So what is this charity?' Lottie stared up at him, her breath short as she matched his sudden hostility.

'The Seraphina Foundation.'

'The Seraphina Foundation?' Lottie's eyes widened, and her heart contracted with the pain of hearing their daughter's name. 'I didn't even know there was such a thing.'

'Well, you've hardly been here to know, have you?' He

shot her a withering look. 'It has actually raised a great deal of money for intensive neonatal care.'

'That's good…'

But it didn't make her feel good. The more she thought about it the more hurt and excluded and resentful she felt that this charity bearing her daughter's name existed and yet she had known nothing about it. It was as if Seraphina had been taken from her, stolen away by Rafael and his team of accountants.

She brushed past Rafael and started up the steps to the *palazzo*. She was being ridiculous—she knew that. How could she be resentful about something that was saving the lives of tiny premature babies? Giving them the chance of life that Seraphina had never had? How could she be so unutterably selfish?

Once inside, Rafael closed the door behind them. 'I imagine you must be tired after the journey.'

It was a statement—something not to be argued with—and certainly no attempt to appease the swing of her mood. His tone of voice made it quite clear that he had no intention of pandering to her obvious strop.

'I have work to do now but I'll let the kitchens know we will need something to eat. Where would you like yours?'

What was it about this place? Palazzo Monterrato? It seemed to Lottie that it refused to let her be happy, that something in the very bricks of the building made it sit up a bit straighter whenever she was around. Like the bored bully in the playground it stubbed out its fag, pushed itself off the wall and decided there was some sport to be had. And Lottie was its favourite target.

It had been raining when she'd woken that morning, splattering against the shuttered windows. And she had been back in 'her' half of their enormous bedroom, alone again in the bed. Only this time she'd felt more alone than ever.

Rafael had not emerged from his office for the rest of the night after their conversation, abandoning her with nothing but a cold supper and a sub-zero mood. She had tried not to be upset—had run herself a bath, taken her book to bed and propped herself up against the pillows, still thinking that he might tap on the door, creep into the room and slide his warm body in next to hers. But she had been deluding herself—as the grey light of this morning pointed out so heartlessly. The bed beside her was still empty, her book was on the floor, where it had slipped from her grasp, and she had nothing but a crick in her neck to show for her misplaced optimism.

And today she had this god-awful dinner to get through.

Pulling on her jeans, she stomped down the two flights of stairs to the kitchens with the idea of making herself a cup of tea. But the place was a hive of activity, the staff in the throes of preparations for this evening, and she was politely told that breakfast would be brought to her, wherever she would like it served.

An hour later her mood had still not improved. Bored with its company, she decided to find someone to share it with and, rapping on the door to Rafael's office, she strode in without waiting for a reply.

'*Sì, verremo più tardi.*' He looked up from his phone conversation, not best pleased at her interruption, judging by the dark scowl on his face. '*Sì—ciao.*' Ending the call, he put down the phone and fixed her with a hooded stare. 'Lottie. Can I help you?'

'Yes, you can, actually.' She wanted to say that he could help her by telling her why he hadn't come to her bed, why she had had to sleep alone again. But there was no way she would give him that satisfaction. No way she would tell him how much she longed to feel his arms around her every single night. Instead she turned to a safer grudge.

'You can tell me what you mean by starting a foundation in Seraphina's name without even telling me.'

Rafael sighed heavily. 'Not this again. I really had no idea that I needed your permission.'

'Well, you did—well, not my permission, but you could have asked…at least told me what you were doing.'

'And would that have made any difference?'

'Yes—yes, it would. If I had known about it I would have felt a part of it. Maybe I could have done some fundraising of my own, in England.'

This produced a derisive snort. 'Do you happen to know many wealthy benefactors?'

Lottie glared at him furiously. 'I do, as a matter of fact. The art world is full of people with more money than they know what to do with. I'm sure I would have been able to get some substantial donations—that's if you had had the courtesy to tell me about it.'

'And what would you have had to do to get these *substantial donations*, I wonder?'

His sneering insinuation made the blood pop in her ears. 'Certainly not what you're suggesting. I have no idea why you think the only way I can get on in the world is by sleeping with wealthy men.'

'Because I am a man, Lottie, and I know how their minds work.'

'Well, you don't know how mine works.'

'That, I'll grant you, is true.' Pressing his fingers to his temples, Rafael leant back in his chair, the bitter expression on his face clearly showing that he wasn't agreeing with her—he was simply acknowledging the disaster of their marriage.

Sitting upright again, he steepled his fingers, looking at

her over the top of them. 'If you are so keen to contribute to the Seraphina Foundation I suggest you make a start by being the perfect hostess tonight. I'm sure you can be charming enough when it's for a good cause. People have paid a lot of money for this event, and there is plenty more where that came from. It will be our job to persuade them to part with it.'

Lottie scowled at him. He might as well have told her to run along and make herself look pretty. Well, she wasn't going to be dismissed that easily. Pulling up a chair, she sat down opposite him, ignoring his dangerously narrowed eyes.

'So tell me about it—the Seraphina Foundation. How long has it been going?'

Rafael sighed heavily again. 'Two years or so.'

'So you started it shortly after I…' Lottie faltered, suddenly wishing she hadn't gone down this line of questioning. 'After I left.'

'Yes.' His look told her that he had no intention of doing anything to ease her discomfort.

'And how much money has it raised?'

'I don't have the exact figures at my fingertips.'

Her silence indicated that she wasn't going to be fobbed off with that.

'It is a considerable sum. People can be very generous with a little persuasion.'

'And where has the money gone? I mean to neonatal units across the principality, or just one particular hospital?

'Originally it was for Ospedale D'Aosta, but now that project has been completed we intend to carry on. There are many other hospitals whose neonatal units desperately need money to update their equipment and facilities and attract the best specialists in that field.'

He stopped abruptly, as if Lottie had tricked him into talking about this.

'Now, if you will forgive me, I have a lot of work to get on with.' Infuriatingly he looked down at his computer. 'I suggest if you need any more information you look at the website.'

Lottie was sorely tempted to tell him what to do with his suggestion. But there was something about the hitch of his shoulders, the very slight unsteadiness in his voice, that held her back. It made her realise that he wasn't purely dismissing her because she irritated the hell out of him— though that was undoubtedly true—but because this was a subject close to his heart…painfully close…and the last thing he wanted was for Lottie so sense his vulnerability.

Well, too bad.

'So Ospedale D'Aosta has all the latest equipment now?'

Just saying the name of the place hurt, and she wrapped her arms around herself for comfort. It was the hospital where Seraphina had been born—where she had died so shortly afterwards.

'That will be useful if I go into premature labour again.'

Rafael's head shot up, and there was a look of such outrage on his face that Lottie's hand flew to her mouth. She wished she could stuff the foolish words back in.

'You won't! You heard what Dr Oveisi said. That despite the accident—what happened—you are no more at risk of a premature birth than anyone else. There is no reason at all for you not to go full-term this time.'

'I know—I know all that, Rafe.'

Lottie watched as he fought back the impulse to say any more. She knew only too well that her default setting was to hide behind flippancy and come out with some stupid comment like that. But she had never expected such a reaction from Rafael. That emotional response had come straight from the heart, from a place buried so deep inside him that she had started to think it didn't exist.

'I'm sure this time everything is going to be fine.' Her throat felt tight with emotion and she swallowed noisily. 'It's not as if the same thing could happen again.'

'No.' Rafael glared savagely at her. 'We can both be sure of that.'

The catastrophic chain of events that had changed their lives so dramatically had started late one summer's day when Rafael had hurried out to the stables to greet a newly arrived horse. Lottie had gone with him, for no other reason than it had been a beautiful summer's evening.

There had been a time when there could be several feral horses pawing and snorting in the stables at Monterrato. Another of Rafael's adrenalin diversions. He had loved the challenge of training those spirited beasts, those wildly unpredictable animals that sometimes even experienced trainers had given up on. Uncharacteristically, he'd seemed to have endless patience with them, and respect too, relishing the thrill of gaining their trust, seeing their fears subside, eventually allowing him to handle them.

That particular evening had seen the arrival of a massive black stallion called Abraxas. Standing some distance away, Lottie had heard the furious clatter of hooves from inside the horsebox, thought she was obeying Rafael's instructions to 'stand the hell back', and had watched as the magnificent beast had bucked and reared down the wooden ramp.

What had happened after that was little more than a blur. With a violent toss of the head and a flash of black, sweaty muscle Abraxas had somehow shaken himself free from the reins held by Rafael and come careering wildly in her direction. The next thing she had known she was curled up on the ground, clutching her swollen stomach, aware that something bad…really bad…had just happened.

Now several long years had passed and the stables stood empty and neglected. But as Rafael and Lottie faced each other in the quiet of the room it was clear that the memory of that savage night still gripped them as brutally as ever.

The helicopter ride to the hospital…the panic and pain of the birth…Rafael striding up and down corridors, powerlessness fuelling his anger as he tried to do something—anything—to end Lottie's agony, to get the baby delivered safely, to save both their lives. And afterwards, when Lottie's life had been out of danger and their tiny, fragile daughter had been fighting for hers, his initial relief had turned to desperate frustration when he'd been told that they didn't have the specialist equipment to save his daughter—that her only hope of survival would be a transfer to another hospital.

He had been on the phone barking out orders, insisting he would take her in his helicopter—had had to be almost physically restrained from scooping up little Seraphina against his broad chest and dashing off with her into the night. But in the end she had proved to be just too small, too weak, and her featherlight grip on life had slipped away before even Rafael could do anything about it.

Getting up, Lottie moved around the desk towards him. She longed more than anything to feel his arms around her, for him to comfort her, to be able to comfort him. She longed for them finally to be able to share their grief instead of having it push them apart, the way it always had.

But, scraping back his chair, Rafael was up on his feet before she had reached him, his arms folded across his chest, his expression dark, forbidding. Everything about the granite set of his jaw, the tight line of his mouth, was telling her to back away, now.

'You need to go now. I have calls to make.'

'Why do you do this, Rafe?' Her voice was choked but she wasn't going to give up. She stood her ground, barring his way, her blue gaze fixed firmly on his face. 'Why do you push me away, lock me out, every time Seraphina is mentioned?'

'I don't know what you are talking about.'

'Yes, you do. You know exactly what I'm talking about. You are doing it right now—look at yourself!' She stood back, theatrically gesturing to him. 'You are virtually ordering me out of the room.'

'I really don't have time for this, Lottie.'

'That's just it, isn't it? You never have time when it comes to talking about Seraphina, about how her death affected us. How are we ever supposed to move on when you flatly refuse to discuss it?'

'There is nothing to discuss. It happened. That is a fact. And no amount of talking is going to change that.'

'And *not* talking about it doesn't make it go away.' She watched as his eyes darkened to black. 'Why don't you try, Rafe? Try to open up? It's got to be better than this...' she stumbled over the words '...this frozen chasm of silence.' Lowering her voice, she fought to control the burn of tears in her throat. 'Why can't you share your feelings with me?'

Taking several paces towards the window, Rafael stopped and turned on his heel to stare at her again, his face a mask of agony. 'Trust me—you wouldn't want to share my feelings.'

'What do you mean by that?'

'I mean that you really wouldn't want to be in my head where Seraphina is concerned.'

'How can you say that?' Lottie was aghast. 'Please Rafe, I'm begging you, just speak honestly with me. Stop shutting me out.'

'Right.' Marching back to the desk, he slammed down the palm of his hand, flashing Lottie a murderous look. 'You have asked, Lottie. You say you want to know my feelings—so here they are.' Sucking in a heavy breath, he jerked back his head, his fists balled by his sides. 'I feel her loss every single day of my life. I feel anger and sadness and bitterness and frustration. But most of all I feel guilt. A deep, abiding guilt that will be with me till the day I die.'

They faced one another in terrible silence.

'There—is that what you wanted to hear? Are you happy now?'

Lottie felt for the edge of the desk to steady herself against a wave of dizziness. 'But it was a tragic accident—you must accept that.' Her voice shook. 'No one was to blame.'

Raising his hand, Rafael silenced her. 'How could I possibly accept that when I was the one who brought the wretched horse to the *palazzo* in the first place? Who was supposed to be responsible for controlling him? I am the one who took you to the wrong damned hospital—who wasn't able to get Seraphina transferred quickly enough.' The pain of his words contorted his beautiful face. 'Need I go on?'

'Stop it, Rafe, you are being ridiculous. It wasn't your fault. It was nobody's fault. No one could have foreseen what would happen.' She reached out to touch him, desperately wanting to be able to ease his misery, but Rafael turned away and her arm was left lowering in mid-air.

'I *am* to blame, Lottie. I *am* responsible for Seraphina's death. And nothing you can say will change that.'

The grand ballroom glittered for the occasion, its enormous chandeliers twinkling above the heads of the noisily chattering guests seated around the dozens of tables.

Waiters moved expertly between them, pouring the finest Monterrato wines into crystal glasses, serving course after course of delicious food. In the background huge floral arrangements lined the walls and a pianist played soft classical music. And seated side by side at the top table were the host and hostess.

Lottie thought the evening was never going to end. She was struggling, really struggling to keep up the façade, when the whole time all she could think about was her earlier conversation with Rafael. His words were going round her head in a continuous loop, muffling the polite questions of the guests on their table, tripping up her hurried answers.

She had been totally amazed by Rafael's bitter confession that he felt responsible for Seraphina's death, was consumed with guilt for what had happened. Why had she never realised this before? But then why *would* she have done? He had always flatly refused to discuss anything to do with Seraphina. And, judging by the way he had sharply dismissed her from his office, he deeply regretted having discussed it now.

She had tried her hardest to play her part, to do her duty—standing beside Rafael with her beautiful oyster silk evening dress sweeping the ground as they greeted the guests, shaking endless hands, air-kissing expensively perfumed cheeks, smiling politely enough for a rictus grin to set in. More than once she had witnessed the raising of a finely shaped eyebrow, the pout of a recently sculpted lip, as the glamorous and good had politely filed past, no doubt itching to get out of earshot and start whispering amongst themselves about the surprise reappearance of the Contessa.

Well, who would have predicted that?

Lottie cast her eyes around the guests at their table

now: a well-known politician, an Italian ambassador, a hugely wealthy investment banker, and their immaculately groomed wives. She wished they would all go home. The wives had soon lost interest in her, turning their attention instead to the gorgeously handsome Conte, each one vying for his attention with decreasing subtlety as the alcohol flowed and the evening wore on.

The banker's wife, Eleanora, seemed particularly determined to flaunt her charms in his direction, leaning forward to touch his hand, purr into his ear, making sure he had the most advantageous view of her expensively acquired cleavage.

Lottie quietly loathed her for it—loathed all of them as she watched them flirting with her husband. But mostly she loathed herself for caring, for allowing her inner green-eyed monster to make an appearance and having it point out to her so eloquently that Rafael should have married one of these glamorous, rich, titled women. How could she ever have been expected to compete with them? Their marriage had been doomed from the start.

To make matters worse, a sideways glance confirmed that Rafael looked particularly stunning tonight, in a dinner suit and black bow tie. Nobody could wear clothes like Rafael, but it wasn't just that; it was his magnetism, the effortless unleashed sex appeal that lay beneath the starched white shirt that turned the eyes of every woman in the room in his direction.

He had been perfectly polite to her all evening—when the attentions of these parasitic women had allowed—but Lottie could sense the cool reserve, the hastily erected impenetrable barrier between them. She could see it as clearly as if it were made of steel.

Finally the evening was over and the last of the guests were escorted to the door to be whisked away in their chauffeur-driven limousines. Lottie was exhausted, but she didn't want to go to bed. She wanted to find Rafael, to talk to him some more, to go over what he had told her and make him see that none of it was his fault.

She found him back in the ballroom, striding tall and dark amongst the post-party debris, thanking the waiting staff individually by name and politely dismissing them. Lottie watched from the doorway as, alone now, he pulled out one of the gilded dining chairs and sat down heavily, stretching out his legs and placing his hands behind his head as he leaned back.

'Rafe?'

Instantly pulling himself upright, he turned to look at her, the chair creaking beneath him. 'Lottie. I thought you had gone to bed.'

'Not yet.' Weaving her way between the tables, Lottie selected a chair and sat down next to him. There was an awkward silence as she rearranged the skirt of her gown. 'I thought the evening went well.'

'Yes—yes, it did.' His undone bow tie lay blackly around his neck, where the top button of his shirt was open. 'Thank you for your part in it. I know you don't find these things easy.'

Lottie bristled. Why was he thanking her as if she was just another member of his staff? And what did he mean about her not finding it easy? Had she looked as awkward as she had felt?

Sitting very straight, she hid behind a mask of dignity. 'Well, I hope I conducted myself appropriately.'

Rafael's dark eyes turned in her direction at the frostiness of her voice.

'Obviously I want to do everything I can to help the Seraphina Foundation. Now that I know it exists, that is.'

'Yes, of course.' He ignored the barb. 'It was a worthy performance.'

Worthy performance?

Heat swept through her body at his derisive, arrogant comment. Taking a deep, controlling breath, she felt the bodice of her gown tighten around her, pushing her breasts upwards.

Rafael looked away.

'And how would you describe *your* performance, then?' she asked.

Rafael's eyes swung back, eyes dangerously dark beneath the sweep of his lashes. 'I did what I had to do.'

'Oh, you did that all right, Rafael. You were lapping up the attention of those fawning women, weren't you? Why don't you admit that you loved every minute of it?' She threw the acid words at him. 'That awful Eleanora woman was virtually climbing inside your trousers and you did nothing to stop her.'

His very Latin shrug of the shoulders had Lottie digging her nails down into her palms. Without using a single word he had managed to convey not only his disregard for her opinion but his contempt for her feelings. Her remarks had been so petty that they weren't even worthy of a reply.

Lottie was still struggling with silent, impotent rage, berating herself for letting this hideously jealous harpy escape, when she heard Rafael getting up from his chair, muttering something softly in Italian under his breath.

'Look, Lottie, why don't we just agree that we have both done our best, that the evening was a success, and leave it at that? Now it's late and you need to go to bed. It's important you don't get overtired.'

Lottie glared at him, fury stinging the backs of her eyes. It was important that she didn't get over-stressed, overwrought, over-bubblingly, seethingly angry too. But he didn't seem to care about *that*.

'And I take it I will be going to bed alone?'

The words escaped before she could stop them and her hand flew, too late, to her mouth. She already knew that Rafael wouldn't be coming to her bed that night. He had made that perfectly clear without the need for any words. Why on earth was she demeaning herself by asking him to say it out loud?

But the shock of her question was totally eclipsed by the devastation of his answer.

'Yes. I have been meaning to talk to you about that. Obviously you are going to need your own space in the *palazzo*. I have arranged for a suite of rooms in the south wing to be made available to you. Your things will be moved there tomorrow.'

Lottie felt her anger seep away, only to be replaced by an emotion a hundred times worse. Like a tidal wave of heartache it swamped her, leaving her feeling weak and breathless and alone—terribly alone. So this was how it was to be. This was Rafael's vision for their future. She was to be locked away for the duration of her pregnancy— exiled like a swelling Mrs Rochester—in the south wing. And after the baby was born...? Who knew what he had planned? Presumably something even more hideous. An island somewhere so remote that he would be able to pretend that she didn't exist at all?

She raised eyes so heavy with sadness that they could hardly bear to look at him, desperately trying to find something in the tight mask of his face, the cold blackness of his eyes, that she could take some comfort from. But there was nothing. Just the twitch of a muscle beneath the scarred cheekbone.

'The south wing, you say?' Her voice was barely more than a whisper in the cavernous quiet of the room.

'That's right. I thought that would be for the best.'

'The best for whom, exactly?'

'For you—for both of us. For all concerned. I think it's important we lay down the ground rules right from the start. So we both know where we stand.'

'Oh, I think you have done that, Rafael.' Lottie bit down hard on her lip to try and stop it trembling. 'Rest assured. I know exactly where I stand.'

Stumbling to her feet, she snatched up a handful of the oyster silk of her gown, turned and fled from the room.

CHAPTER ELEVEN

LOTTIE OPENED HER eyes to the cold reality of a new day. Going into the bathroom, she held her hair back with one hand as she splashed cold water onto her face, roughly rubbing it dry before returning to the bedroom and looking around her.

She had made her decision and she was strangely calm. She was leaving. Leaving Monterrato and leaving Rafael. And this time there would be no going back.

She had spent the night thinking everything through as clearly as she could. Staring at the tangled mess of their relationship, she had forced herself to try and unravel it, following the thread, carefully picking away at the knots, refusing to stop no matter how painful it had been.

And the more she had unravelled the more obvious it had been. Rafael wanted her solely for one thing. To bear him an heir. She had known that right from the start—he had been brutally honest about it. But somehow the truth had got lost along the way, obscured by the fanciful notions insidiously creeping in, fooling her into thinking that he might actually have some feelings for her, that there might even be a chance of them reuniting as a couple.

But last night all those notions had been cruelly dispelled. Rafael's vision for the future left no room for any silly ideas about happy families. And the truth hurt—more than hurt. It was an agony that would never, ever go away. Because when it came down to it that was all they had, she and Rafael, the one true constant that she could always rely on with their relationship. Pain. And hurt. And that was all Lottie could feel now.

But she knew she had to use that pain to give her the strength to leave now. Because strength was the only language Rafael understood—the only way to fight him. If she showed any weakness, let him see her true feelings, he would use them, twist them to his advantage, ensure that she would never be free of him. She had to be strong—for herself and the baby. He would always be its father—of course he would—but that didn't give him the right to blight the rest of her life. Because that was how it would be if she stayed here. Nothing more than a half-life, constantly tormented by the love she had for him—a love that he would never return.

Walking around the bedroom, she gathered up her belongings, stuffing them into her suitcase. She picked up the oyster silk dress, holding it at arm's length, watching the way the fabric shimmered down to the ground. Then, folding it over her arm, she took it over to the armoire and placed in on a hanger beside the other beautiful dresses that she would never wear again.

She caught sight of her reflection as she closed the mirrored door, shocked for a moment by what she saw: the dark circles under her eyes, the unnatural pallor of her skin. Yes, this was what Rafael Revaldi had done to her. Jutting out her chin, she attempted a defiant stance, balling her fists by her sides, practising the measured, authoritative way she would tell Rafael of her decision.

Just thinking about confronting him made her feel physically faint, but she knew it had to be done and it had to be done now. Whilst she still had the strength to go through with it.

Descending the staircase, Lottie strained to see if she could hear Rafael's voice anywhere in the *palazzo*, but the only sounds came from the ballroom, where the cleaning up operation was obviously in progress.

He wasn't in his office, or the dining room, nor in the grand salon or indeed the ballroom. Feeling increasingly sick, Lottie hurried outside. Standing at the top of the steps, she shielded her eyes from the low sun, scanning the calm vista with a thumping heart, as if Rafael might be about to jump out from behind a poplar tree at any moment.

She ran down the steps, round to the back of the *palazzo*, searching everywhere, anywhere she thought he might possibly be, getting increasingly frantic when there was still no sign of him. Where the hell *was* he? She could feel panic creeping over her, its icy fingers wrapping around her chest, restricting her breathing.

Finding herself at the edge of the woodland area, she stopped and took in a shuddering breath. A breeze had picked up and it whipped the hair across her face, catching it on her open lip, blurring her vision.

She would go to the graveyard. Go and see Seraphina—take a few minutes to calm herself down, gather her strength.

She shivered as she walked through the woods towards the chapel. The weak sunlight offered no heat as it filtered through the framework of bare trees. Finally reaching Seraphina's grave, she slumped against the devoted angel, feeling the cold of the marble seeping into her bones. She wasn't sure how long she'd leant there before a sudden noise had her heart thumping in her chest.

'Lottie!' Suddenly Rafael appeared from nowhere, crashing towards her. 'What the hell are you doing here?'

Lottie jerked herself upright, swamped by anger, dread, and most of all pain at the sight of him.

'I came to spend some time at our daughter's grave.' She threw back her head, the wind catching her hair again, lifting it from her shoulders. 'Not that it is any of your business.'

'Your irresponsible behaviour is making this my business.' He sounded black with temper. '*Per l'amor di Dio*, you haven't even got a coat on!' What are you trying to do? Make yourself ill?'

Before she could reply he was beside her, tugging off his jacket and flinging it over her shoulders.

'*Dio*, you are freezing—come here.' He pressed her against his chest, wrapping his strong arms around her, rubbing her back through the waxed cotton fabric of the jacket.

'Get off me.' Her voice was muffled against his shirt and she wriggled herself free from him, stumbling round to the other side of Seraphina's grave from where she glared aggressively at him. 'Leave me alone.'

Rafael glared back, mystified. 'What's the matter with you?' And then, as a terrible thought occurred to him, his voice dropped. 'Is everything all right?'

'Yes.' Lottie forced herself to hold his stare. 'If by that you mean the baby, everything is fine.'

Relief flooded Rafael's eyes, but seconds later they darkened again. 'So what, then? What are you doing here? What is going on?'

His questions shot at her like rapid gunfire.

'Why are you behaving like this?'

'I can behave however I want.'

'No, you can't. Not if it puts my child at risk.' His voice was raw, clear and cold. 'When it comes to protecting my baby's life, you will do exactly as I say.'

'Oh, you think so, do you?' Lottie matched his anger with her own. 'Well that is where you are wrong. As a matter of fact I have been looking for you.' The warning look in Rafael's eyes threatened to steal her courage but she blundered on. 'To tell you that I am going back home—to England.' She could feel her heart pounding frantically behind her ribs at the enormity of what she was saying. 'For good.'

There was a beat of silence between them, pierced by the single caw of a raven overhead.

'No. You are not.' Rafael's voice was dangerously quiet, his eyes burning with fire.

'Yes.' Lottie squared up to him as best she could, shivering violently beneath his jacket. 'I've made up my mind.'

'Well, you can just unmake it.' The lash of his words whistled across at her. 'I can assure you, Charlotte, you are doing no such thing.'

'You can't stop me, Rafael. I'm going to go back to England and have the baby there and—'

'Charlotte, if you think, for one tiny second, that I would let you leave the country, take our baby away, then you have seriously misjudged me.' His breath escaped in angry puffs of condensed air. 'What's all this about anyway?' The depth of his scowl all but closed his eyes. 'What is going on?'

'I've told you what is going on. I've made up my mind and I am returning to England.'

Rafael shook his head, fury slowing the movement. 'And I am saying you are doing no such thing. I have no idea what has brought this on, but I do know that you can stop this nonsense right now. My baby will be born here and will be raised here—by its father—at the Palazzo Monterrato.'

He hesitated, his scowl turning to a sneer.

'You have run away once and I'm sure you are capable of doing that again. Should you choose to leave after the baby is born, then so be it. But the baby will stay here. And for the time being you are going *nowhere*.'

The word resonated with ruthless force.

Lottie fought to control hot tears of fury and despair. His words were like a fish hook in her flesh. The more she struggled the worse the pain. If she had wanted proof of his feelings for her she had it right there. *Should you choose to leave after the baby is born, then so be it.* She meant nothing to him—nothing at all. Without the baby she might as well not exist.

Biting back the searing pain, she rounded on him, using anger to mask the agony, covering her misery with its red cloak.

'I'm sure you would *love* that, wouldn't you?' She spat the words at him. 'Once the baby has been born there is nothing you would like better than for me to disappear completely.'

Rafael stared at her. 'What are you talking about?'

'I'm talking about you—me—the whole ridiculous idea that we could ever live together, have any sort of meaningful relationship, baby or no baby.'

'Look...' Making a visible effort now, Rafael lowered his tone, inched towards her as if dealing with one of his feral horses. 'I don't know what this is all about, but maybe if you were to just calm down...'

He stretched out an arm towards her but she batted it away furiously, the jacket sliding off her shoulders.

'It's about the fact that I mean nothing to you—*nothing*! I am no more than a surrogate—worse than a surrogate. Because you can't just pay me off and forget about me. Instead you have to lock me away in some far-flung corner of the *palazzo*. But I am your last, your *only* chance of providing an heir for Monterrato and you hate me for it. Don't even try and deny it.'

Her voice was reaching a harridan screech as it picked up speed, denying Rafael any sort of reply.

'If it hadn't been for your accident you would have been rid of me for good. You would have carried on living your self-indulgent bachelor lifestyle for as long as you liked, eventually choosing a suitable mother for your precious children when the fancy took you from any number of painted, perfect, pouting women like the ones who were fawning all over you last night.'

A cold quiet descended as Lottie gulped in a shuddering, juddering breath that racked through her whole body.

Rafael just stared at her.

'So is that what this is about? This ridiculous behaviour?' Realisation coloured his words. 'Some petty rivalry with the women at the dinner last night? Perhaps you should be careful, Lottie.' His eyes glittered coldly, his voice suddenly terrifyingly soft. 'We wouldn't want to misinterpret this little outburst as a fit of *jealousy*, would we? Fool ourselves into thinking that you actually *care*. We both know better than that. Perhaps I need to remind you that who I see, who I take to my bed—'

'Stop!' With a piercing scream Lottie covered her ears. 'I don't want to hear any more.'

'Is none of your business.' His rapier tongue hadn't finished with her yet. 'You left me...remember?'

His words floated across the stillness of their daughter's grave. Across the great chasm of misunderstanding and pain that had blighted their lives.

'It's not something I am likely to forget.' Washed with grief, Lottie's words were barely audible.

That lie—that terrible lie. *'I don't love you Rafael, and*

I never have.' Delivered in a moment of tortured panic and accepted, just like that, as brutal, irrevocable fact.

'Well, that makes two of us.' He gave a derisive snort. 'You had me fooled, Lottie, I'll give you that. I had no idea—no idea at all—that that was coming. Idiot that I was, I thought we were for ever—imagine that? And all the time I meant nothing to you—you were desperate to be rid of me. When you finally came out with the fact that you had never loved me, well...' He stopped, his throat moving as if he had swallowed something sharp. 'If you want the truth, I will tell you. It crucified me, Lottie, totally crucified me.'

This was more than Lottie could bear. Her own pain she could cope with. She *had* to cope with. But seeing the suffering that twisted the muscles of Rafael's beautiful face made something snap inside her.

'I lied.'

'*Chiedo scusa?* I beg your pardon?'

'I lied, Rafe. When I said I didn't love you.' Her voice was very small.

'*Sì*, right—of course you did. I was there, Lottie, I heard you say the words, saw the look in your eyes as you spoke them.'

'I lied because I had to—because I knew it was the only way you would let me go.'

'*Che diavolo*?' Rafael snarled at her. 'If this is some misguided way of trying to make me feel better then don't bother.'

'You were talking about telling the truth—well, this is my truth. When I said what I said it was for your benefit, so you would be free of me.'

'How very kind.' The sarcasm in his voice was chilling. 'And why exactly would I want to be free of you?'

'Because our marriage was a mess—nothing but endless trips to fertility clinics and failed IVF attempts. Because I saw no reason for Seraphina's death to ruin both our lives.' Lottie gulped in a breath of cold air. 'I thought if I left I could take the pain of Seraphina's death away with me. That you would be better off without me.'

Fury contorted Rafael's face. 'Don't you *dare* bring Seraphina into this. You have never had the sole rights to that pain, no matter what you might think. She was *my* daughter, *my* little girl, every bit as much as she was yours, and I felt the pain of her loss—still feel the pain of her loss—every bit as deeply as you. More so, in fact, as I shoulder the guilt for her death.'

'Well, I didn't know that then. How could I have done when you refused to ever speak of her?' Her words were squeezed out between strangled sobs. 'I felt like I was grieving totally on my own.'

'How dare you say that?'

'I needed your support but you thought about nothing but producing another baby. It was like an obsession—as if without a baby there was no point to our marriage, no point in our staying together.'

'That's the most preposterous thing I have ever heard.'

'And when it didn't happen…when all the drugs and doctors and clinics failed…I knew that I had failed. I felt depressed and empty and useless.' Deflated now, she reached out to the angel beside her for support, to stop herself sliding to the ground.

'*Dio*, Lottie.' Rafael looked as if a part of his body had started to hurt. 'Don't you realise that I was trying to be strong? Watching you grieve broke my heart. The last thing I wanted was to make it worse by showing you my pain.'

Lottie sniffed loudly, trying hard to hang on, not to collapse in a pool of misery. 'Don't *you* realise that you made it a million times worse by not showing me your pain? If we had been a proper couple we would have grieved together and then thought about trying for another baby when the time was right. But that wasn't how it was. Getting me pregnant again was all that mattered to you.'

'No, Lottie, I won't have this. I won't have you rewriting the past. I was trying to rescue what was left of the disaster that I had caused. I was responsible for the death of our baby, for the fact that you could never conceive naturally again. I had to try and put things right as best I could. That is the truth of the matter.'

'Well, that may be your truth, but that was not how it felt to me.' The anguish twisting inside her like a corkscrew gave Lottie the strength to go on. 'To me it felt as if you'd only married me because I was pregnant. And when we lost Seraphina you realised it had all been a mistake, that you were stuck with me for no reason. That was why you were so determined to get me pregnant again—to justify our marriage to yourself.'

'Dio!' Rafael turned from her, stamping a couple of paces away before swinging round again. 'I don't believe I am hearing this. I can only assume you have concocted this ridiculous story to try and make yourself feel better. To ease your guilt you have somehow convinced yourself that it was all my fault—that I was the one to blame when you walked out on our marriage.'

'It's not a question of blame. I never said it was your fault. I'm trying to explain why I said what I did.'

'So by telling me that you had never loved me, by sneaking away in the night without even having the guts to tell me what you were doing, you were actually doing me a *favour?* You were freeing me from the chains of marital responsibility?' He shook his head with vitriolic disbelief.

'Yes.'

'Nothing to do with the fact that you wanted out of our relationship? That you had had enough of me?'

'No, nothing to do with that.'

'And you expect me to believe that?'

'Yes, because it's the truth. And I was right. You *have* led a better life without me. You have moved on…formed new relationships. If it hadn't been for your accident you would never have had to see me again.'

'Don't you *dare* tell me how I have led my life.' Rafael looked as if he was about to explode. 'You know nothing, Charlotte—*nothing.*'

'I know that you didn't come after me. Try to get me back.'

Incredulity raged in his eyes. 'After what you'd said to me?' He couldn't bear to look at her. 'There is such a thing as pride, you know. I was hardly going to beg. I can control most things in my life, but even I can't make someone love me.'

Suddenly the tears were streaming uncontrollably down Lottie's face. 'You didn't need to make me love you, Rafe. I have always loved you.' She covered her face with her hands, and her voice was muffled through her wet fingers. 'And I always will.'

CHAPTER TWELVE

RAFAEL STARED AT the forlorn figure shivering on the other side of Seraphina's grave. She looked so vulnerable, so fragile, standing there, her cold hands trembling in front of her face. Every fibre of his being wanted to go to her, to wrap his arms around her and hold her tight. To tell her that he could make everything better. But he couldn't.

Lottie's revelation that she had lied to him that night had knocked him sideways. It couldn't be true. The cruel way she had said those words, the look on her face when she'd delivered them, had left no room for doubt. She had meant them, all right. Now she had let time take her words and shape them into something more palatable, mould them into a convenient lie that would assuage her conscience.

Well, he wasn't falling for that—he wasn't going to let her hurt him again.

He could still feel the searing pain of her cruel statement, even after all this time, and that gave him strength. The strength he so badly needed to stop himself from reaching out to her, from holding her tearstained face in his hands, from raising her lips to meet his and kissing away the heartache of this whole wretched business.

'Aren't you going to say anything?'

Lottie's anguished voice cut through the silence and she gazed, petrified, across at him.

'What is there to say?'

Rafael turned his head away. He couldn't bear to look at her—knew that if he did he would weaken, that all the resolve he had built up over the last two years would be swept away in the tidal wave of emotion that the very sight of her beautiful tortured face threatened to unleash.

'You obviously think you know it all already. You have brutally choreographed my life without ever actually asking me if that was what *I* wanted.'

His livid gaze swept across the overgrown graves.

'Had you done so you would have known that you couldn't have been more wrong. I never viewed our marriage purely in terms of having children. However...' He allowed himself a quick glance in her direction, saw the tears that were silently rolling down her cheeks, dripping off her chin. He had to keep strong. 'If it makes you feel better to think that, if it eases some of the guilt you presumably felt, then go ahead—be my guest. It's not as if any of it matters any more. Just don't expect me to believe you.'

'Rafe!' Lottie uttered his name with a strangled cry. 'I am just trying to explain how I felt, that's all—explain why I left you.'

'Well, don't bother.' As he raised his hand to silence her his eyes were jet-black. 'It's way too late for that. I was taken in by you once, Charlotte. It's not going to happen again.'

Twisting away from her, he jammed his hands into his jeans pockets and kicked at the moss-covered path.

'I'm going back to the *palazzo* now. I suggest you do the same. Freezing to death out here is not going to solve anything.'

Lottie watched as his tall figure turned and marched its way between the ancient gravestones. At the top of the steps he paused, turning back to look at her, his anger channelled into uncompromising authority.

'And don't even think about running away again, Lottie.' His words cut through the cold air. 'I will be watching you.'

Back at the *palazzo* Rafael crashed into his office, kicking the door shut behind him. Away from the pitiful sight of Lottie, he felt the anger kicking in, slowly building and building until it threatened to engulf him completely. He had never felt like this before, so consumed with frustrated bile.

Turning on the computer, he realised his hands were shaking as they hovered over the keyboard. How could she talk about running away? *Again.* How dared she do this to him? And this time she was carrying his child, for God's sake. His chest heaved with the fury and injustice of it all.

He logged on to his email, desperately looking for a distraction to steady his heart-rate, regulate his breathing, stop him from marching out and doing something really stupid. Like finding Lottie again and demanding that she stayed here, with him. Not just for now, not until after the baby was born, not even for the next twenty years while they watched their child become an adult. He wanted to make her swear that she would stay with him for ever.

His mind flashed back to the dinner last night, the agony of sitting beside her all evening. She had looked so enchanting in that silk gown, the pale colour against her skin giving her an ethereal beauty, a tenderness that had made him want to both protect her and ravish her— not necessarily in that order. She had somehow twisted her hair into a plait over the top of her head, fastening it in a bun at the back. And with the violet earrings he had given her catching the light in her eyes he had never seen her look more beautiful.

He had known then, more forcefully than ever, that his decision to move her to the south wing was the right one. If he had any chance of holding on to his sanity he was going to have to keep away from her. Or keep her away from him.

He had woken this morning knowing that something was wrong, fear clutching at his heart, tightening its grip when, hours later, there had still been no sign of Lottie. Eventually he had given in to temptation and knocked on her door, but had expressly forbidden himself from looking in when there was no answer. Instead he had charged around the *palazzo* and its grounds looking for her, finally tracking her down at their daughter's grave. Only to hear the devastating revelation that she was leaving.

Like hell she was.

Rafael took in a heavy breath and, leaning forward, made himself concentrate on the growing string of emails. There was one from Dr Oveisi's office, asking for information regarding Contessa Revaldi's embryo transplant. Had she done a pregnancy test yet? Rafael quickly composed a brief affirmative message, saying that the Contessa was indeed pregnant.

Pregnant. Somehow now the news was leaking out it seemed more real. Lottie was pregnant and he was going to be a father. He should have been ecstatic, euphoric. When he had been lying in that hospital bed, adjusting to the devastating news that he was sterile, it had been all he could think about. The fact that he did have one last chance to be a father. He had plotted and schemed to achieve his goal and now it had worked just the way he had been determined it would.

So how had he ended up feeling like this? Why did his body hurt more now than it had when he had woken up from that damned accident, battered, bruised and broken?

Because of Lottie—that was why.

* * *

Lottie stood perfectly still, the clouds scudding across the sky above her. She couldn't move, frozen, numbed to the core, by her harrowing confrontation with Rafael.

She had known that telling him she was leaving would be the hardest thing she had ever had to do in her whole life. Last time she had taken the coward's way—*'sneaking away in the night'*, as Rafael's words had so painfully reminded her. This time she had had to do it face to face. She had foolishly tried to tell herself that she would be able to convince him, make Rafael see sense, that it was the only practical solution. That they could never live together, even in a place as huge as the *palazzo*, even if she was exiled to the south wing…

But nothing had prepared her for the onslaught of misery that had just happened. Never, in her most deranged of moments, had she ever envisaged admitting to him that she still loved him. Whatever could possibly have possessed her to do that? Had something deep in her subconscious persuaded her that he might say the same, say that he loved her too, that they could be together for ever? If so her subconscious deserved to die a long and painful death. Because now she no longer even had the one thing left she could call her own. Her pride. That lay in tatters at her feet, along with her shredded declaration of love for him and the gruesome mess that was her bleeding heart.

Lottie bent down and picked up Rafael's jacket, slipping her arms into the oversized sleeves, pulling it close around her, her body still shaking uncontrollably beneath it.

She had to leave. There was no doubt about that. Somehow she had to find the strength to explain to Rafael, coldly and clearly, why it was impossible for her to stay.

* * *

Pacing savagely round his office, Rafael stopped in front of the window. He had never felt like this before. So close to losing control. It was as if everything he thought he knew—everything about his character, his life—was being challenged. And found wanting.

He had been so protective of his own pride that he had refused to listen to Lottie, refused to let himself open up to her. Why had he not even considered that what she had just told him might be true? That maybe he *had* handled things badly after Seraphina died. That maybe he hadn't taken time to grieve. That maybe, just maybe, she *did* still love him.

And what the hell did he think he was doing now? Shutting himself away in his office when she was out there somewhere, hurting? Lottie—the woman who was pregnant with his baby, the woman who meant more to him than anything in the world. One thing was for sure: if he let her slip through his fingers again he would never forgive himself. He had to do something about it now. Before it was too late.

They collided in the hallway. Lottie, running in from outside, coming up against the steel wall of Rafael's chest. As his arms went out to steady her she pushed herself away and they stood there, facing each other, for several long, silent seconds.

'I was just coming to look for you.' Lottie brushed back the wild mess of curls from her face, from cold cheeks that were streaked with tears. She forced herself to meet his eyes, to squeeze the words past her closing throat. 'To tell you that I'm sorry, Rafael, so sorry...but I meant what I said about...'

'About having always loved me?'

She stopped dead.

'About…about…' she stammered, eyes wide with confusion, her heart swerving in her chest. 'About having to leave.'

His eyes were scanning her face with such intensity it felt as if he was searching her soul for the truth. But she mustn't falter now—not when she had got this far. She sucked in a breath, feeling it shudder down the length of her body. Somehow she had to find the strength to carry on, force the jagged words out of her mouth. Then it would be done.

'We both know I can't stay here, Rafael. I will return to Monterrato in time to have the baby, of course, and then we can work out the best way to proceed after that.'

There—it was said. She allowed her gaze to slide to the floor.

'Did you mean it, Lottie? When you said you had always loved me?'

The black and white squares of marble blurred beneath her feet. Why was he doing this to her? She was waiting for anger, denial, refusal, bracing herself for more of the blind rage that he had showed her earlier. She could cope with that. But this…? This was a far more excruciating form of torture.

'Yes.' Her voice was very small.

Tipping up her chin with his finger, Rafael locked his eyes on hers again. 'So when you walked out…when you said those words to me…?' He faltered, drinking in the violet-blue of her eyes, still searching for the answer, sure that it had to be held in there somewhere.

'It was a lie, Rafe. The biggest lie of my life.'

'And now? This is the truth?'

As he removed his finger from her chin Lottie realised that his hand was shaking.

'Yes—yes, Rafael, it is. This is the truth.'

'Then say it,' he growled from somewhere deep in his throat. 'Say the words, Lottie.'

Lottie gazed upwards, scanning his scarred, handsome face as if for the last time, before surrendering to the force in his eyes.

'I love you, Rafael.'

Lowering his head, Rafael brushed his mouth against hers, capturing her words with his lips, holding them, tasting them, letting the truth in all its naked glory pass from her body to his.

With aching tenderness the pressure of his kiss increased, until it flooded through Lottie's body like warm water, melting her against him, washing away everything else that had ever passed between them. Closing her eyes, she let herself float away. If this was their final parting kiss, then so be it—she would give herself up to it, surrender to the glorious feeling that obliterated every other thought. And remember it for ever.

Finally she felt Rafael's lips leave hers, felt him loosen his hold on her, and knew she was going to have to open her eyes to the cold reality of the future. She waited, looking up into his dark returning stare. There was an agonising pause before he lifted his hands, cupped them around her face and looked deep, deep into her eyes.

'*Anch'io ti amo*. I love you too, Lottie.'

Pulling apart at last, they moved into the salon. Rafael bent to put a match to the fire prepared in the hearth, then drew Lottie back beside him as they watched as the flames licked around the kindling, crackling it into life.

As he turned to look down at her his dark eyes were brimming with love in a way that Lottie had never, ever thought she would see again. Then he wrapped his arms around her and pulled her into the tightest hug.

'It will warm up in a minute.'

'I'm not cold.'

How could she be, locked in his arms, with his astonishing words still resonating in her head?

'Good.' He paused, running a hand over her tangled curls, tracing the shape of her skull with the flat of his palm. 'I'm so sorry, Lottie.'

'No.' Moving away just enough to look up at his face, Lottie stopped him. 'I should be saying sorry, not you. I'm the one who ran away, who didn't have the courage to tell you to your face how I felt.'

'I didn't give you the chance.' Drawing her back against his chest, he spoke the words softly over her head. 'I was so consumed with guilt...'

He resisted the pull of Lottie against him.

'No, let me say this—I have to say this. I was so consumed with guilt over Seraphina's death that it took over everything in my life. I refused to grieve, refused to even let myself witness your grief, because it twisted the knife in my heart still further. Every time I looked at you it was like a permanent reminder of what I had done—to our baby, to you. I thought I had taken away from you the only thing that mattered.'

'No, of course you hadn't, Rafe.' Forcibly loosening herself from the grip of his arms, Lottie tipped back her head to look at him. 'That wasn't how it was at all. You have to stop tormenting yourself.'

'So instead I made it my mission to try and change that terrible destiny. And when it didn't happen, when the IVF didn't work, instead of standing back and taking a long hard look at what I was doing, instead of devoting myself to trying to make you happy, I turned into some crazed adrenalin junkie, pushing myself further and further physically and further and further away from you.'

He stopped abruptly, the glitter of tears in his eyes. 'Can you ever forgive me, Lottie?'

'Rafael.' Shrugging off his arms, she raised her hands to his face, brushing away the dark curls from his forehead, grazing her fingers against the ridge of the scar. 'Listen to me.'

He had no option now but to meet her gaze, see that what she was saying was the truth. 'You were *not* responsible for Seraphina's death. Do you hear me?'

'But if I had taken you to the hospital in Milan... They had better equipment there—they might have saved her...'

'It was a much longer journey, Rafe. I might have given birth in the helicopter, and even if I hadn't Seraphina would almost certainly have died. She was just too premature, Rafe. Too tiny...too frail. You have to accept that. You did everything you could. But ultimately what happened was beyond your control.' She gazed at his beautiful agonised face, desperate to take away the pain, to make him see that he wasn't to blame. She lowered her voice gently. 'Even *you* can't control everything, you know, Rafe.'

'That I do know.' Rafael's huff of acceptance finally released some of the tension and a smile touched his lips. 'I can't control my feelings for you. I tried to stop loving you, Lottie—*Dio*, how I tried. But no matter what you did, no matter how much I reminded myself that you had walked out on me, that you had never loved me, I couldn't stop the love I had for you. And I hated myself for it.'

'I'm so sorry...'

Rafael brought his lips down on hers for another silencing kiss. 'No more sorries. No more regrets. We have made a mess of the past but now we have the whole of our future to put things right. And it starts here.'

He took hold of her hand and Lottie watched as he placed it on her abdomen, resting his own over the top.

Then their eyes met again with the miraculous realisation. They were a family already: Rafael, Lottie and the baby. Everything was going to be fine.

The fire crackled and popped in celebration.

EPILOGUE

Last night Contessa Charlotte Revaldi, wife of Conte Rafael Revaldi, gave birth to a son, Valentine Rafael John, at Ospedale D'Aosta.

As the Conte di Monterrato arrived to visit mother and baby this morning he announced that they were both doing extremely well and that he and his wife couldn't be more proud of their longed-for second child—a brother for Seraphina.

The couple's first child tragically died three years ago after a premature birth. A steady stream of friends and well-wishers have been visiting the hospital all day, with flowers and gifts for the happy family.

PUTTING THE NEWSPAPER down on the hospital bed, Lottie looked across at Rafael, who was cradling their baby in his arms, rocking slightly from side to side as he gazed into his son's sleeping face. They looked so right together, a perfect fit, with that small bundle of life snuggled against the powerfully muscled arms of his father. The present and the future. Lottie could already see the trouble they were going to cause her. And she couldn't wait.

'I meant to say, my mother rang this morning to congratulate us.'

'Greta? That was nice of her.'

'Yes, I was quite surprised, actually. I'd never really thought of her as granny material, but she seemed genuinely excited. She's even talking about paying us a visit.'

'I'll have to practise my best behaviour.' Rafael gave her a schoolboy grin over the top of the baby's head, leaving Lottie in no doubt that her mother would be totally charmed by him.

'And Alex, of course—she's been on the phone, demanding photos of Valentine and all the gruesome birth details. I think I've managed to put her off the idea of ever having a baby.'

'Some friend you are.' Rafael laughed. 'But, seriously, you were magnificent, Lottie. I can't tell you how proud I am of you.'

'That's because I had you there with me. And I would do it a thousand times over—because look what we got.' She tipped her head on one side.

'I can't stop looking.' Rafael returned his gaze to his son and there was a tender pause. 'I think he takes after you, you know—those beautiful wide eyes. And look at his tiny nose, and his lips, and his little ears.'

'So you approve, then?'

As he glanced up again Lottie saw that his eyes were shining with emotion, and when she saw his slight shake of the head and deep swallow she knew he was struggling to find the words.

'I can still hardly believe it. That he is really ours, Lottie, yours and mine.'

'Well, you'd better believe it. Especially when he is screaming his head off at three in the morning. And Valentine looks more like *you*, just for the record. That certainly isn't *my* hair!'

Rafael protectively smoothed his hand over his son's

shock of dark hair, then watched as it sprang back to up-right. 'Listen to your *mamma*, being rude about your hair. You and I both know you are perfect in every way.'

'He really is…' Lottie sighed with exhausted pleasure and laid her head back on the pillow. 'We did good, didn't we?'

'We did more than good.'

Sitting on the edge of the bed with the baby in his arms, he leant forward to kiss Lottie tenderly on the lips.

'We did *assolutamente magnifico*. And this is just the start, Lottie—the start of a wonderful life together: you, me and our son. A proper family at last. Now and for ever.

* * * * *

MILLS & BOON®

Want to get more from Mills & Boon?

Here's what's available to you if you join the exclusive **Mills & Boon eBook Club** today:

✦ *Convenience – choose your books each month*

✦ *Exclusive – receive your books a month before anywhere else*

✦ *Flexibility – change your subscription at any time*

✦ *Variety – gain access to eBook-only series*

✦ *Value – subscriptions from just £1.99 a month*

So visit **www.millsandboon.co.uk/esubs** today to be a part of this exclusive eBook Club!

MILLS & BOON®

MODERN™

POWER, PASSION AND IRRESISTIBLE TEMPTATION